SINFUL RESTRAINT

THEIR BABYDOLL COLLECTION
BOOK 1

CALISTA JAYNE

Daddies' Girl

Daddies' Babydoll

by Calista Jayne

ABOUT THE BOOK

Calling one man "daddy" is naughty enough—but two?

My creepy ex keeps popping up everywhere I turn.

My apartment is in shambles.

My life is spiraling out of control.

But a steamy encounter with not one but two commanding men shows me that maybe it's time to let someone else—or two someone elses—take care of me.

They have extreme expectations for what it means to be theirs...but after one taste of the pleasure they dole out, I'm hooked. I'll do anything, as long as they'll call me their babydoll.

This set includes the first two episodes of the Their Babydoll series.

Contents include: daddy kink, MFM sexytimes, spanking, BDSM, kidnapping by bad guys, violence and mental abuse by bad guys.

DADDIES' GIRL

PROLOGUE

Olivia

The dream is almost too real. Lips trail across my skin, creating a path of heat from my throat, between my breasts, down to my navel. And then lower.

I gasp and reach down to guide the man where I want him, where I *need* him. His lips encircle my clit and he sucks gently before kissing his way down my pussy and licking the slit. His tongue slides in and I moan, helpless against his wicked mouth. He presses a finger inside of me, and then a second one, and I'm writhing against him, chasing my orgasm.

My phone vibrates next to me, waking me up.

Crap. That's hardly fair. I wake with a start and find myself lying half across the rickety desk in my university-assigned art studio. The studio isn't much to look at, but as a senior at San Esteban School of the Arts, having my own studio is something I've earned.

And being surrounded by my own sculptures? It's an amazing feeling.

My phone buzzes again, and I look at the screen.

Daniel: *I'm heading to your place with takeout. Come home soon or I'll eat it all.*

I smile and text him back. *Is it from the taco place I like?*

Daniel: *Nah, I didn't feel like tacos. I got Subathon.*

Olivia: *Okay, thanks.*

I won't be in a rush to get home, then. Subathon sells cheap fast-food sandwiches, and while I don't mind the idea of cheap and fast, Daniel knows very well I got food poisoning last time he picked up dinner there. But if I complain, he'll throw a hissy fit, so I wake up my laptop and try to get back to work. I'm definitely not in a rush to return to the apartment—he can eat both sandwiches, for all I care.

As I stare at the blank document on my laptop's screen, the sculpture behind it captures my attention. *I* made that beautiful thing. It still surprises me, sometimes, to look at it.

The spiraling arches are made of two abstract forms. It's more sensual than I'd originally intended—it reminds me of two lovers in an embrace. Three, actually, because of the shadows formed by the arches. I wonder if the sculpture is responsible for that crazy-hot dream I was in the middle of. Damn, I need to get laid. Maybe I'll get lucky tonight and Daniel won't be passed out in front of the TV when I get home.

Then again, I doubt he could do what that faceless guy in my dreams was doing. Getting head from Daniel is rare, but to be honest, I don't encourage it because he acts like it's a huge favor to me.

Not for the first time, I wonder why we're still together. I wonder if I should break things off.

But then who would I be left with?

AN HOUR PASSES. Daniel texts again just as I'm starting a new paragraph on my final project essay. I ignore my phone and try to recapture the thought.

He texts once more, and I glance at my phone.

Daniel: *Where are you?*

Jeez, give me a minute. The sentence in my head is right there, so close to my consciousness. Writing doesn't come easily to me, and I had it—

Daniel: *What the fuck, Olivia? Where are you?*

Giving up on my essay, I text back, *I'm at the studio, trying to write my paper.*

Daniel: *You can do that at the apartment.*

Olivia: *Too many distractions.*

Daniel: *I'll be quiet, promise. Need you here, O.*

Sighing, I pack up my laptop. I should just leave it here in my studio, because I know there isn't the slimmest chance I'll be able to work at my apartment, not with Daniel there, either hovering or watching television. But maybe when he leaves for work in the morning—a cushy, paid internship at his parents' company—I'll get some time to concentrate on my final essay.

As I walk to my car, which is parked on the far side of campus, I'm not thinking about my essay, my sculpture, or my boyfriend. I'm thinking about that dream. I can't remember what the guy looked like or if my dream even gave him a face other than the lips and tongue that lapped at my pussy.

It wasn't just the sexiness of it, either. There was something about the way he licked and kissed me, like it was his life calling. Like he *treasured* me. Like he wanted to take care of me.

But that sort of thing is imaginary. Nobody could care that much.

~

Jaxon

I know it's a dream because in real life, I'm single, and I haven't touched a woman in weeks. But there's a woman in front of me. On her hands and knees. Brown hair. A plump, smackable ass, which I'm currently framing with my hands on her hips as I thrust into her pussy.

Damn, she feels good, her cunt so snug on my cock.

She makes desperate moaning sounds. "More, Daddy, please," she begs.

"I've got you, Babydoll," I say, grunting with the desire to come, but the need to hold back until she finds her own release.

That's new. I don't usually give pet names to my sexual partners right away. They have to earn it, usually after several hook-ups. Maybe I'm dreaming of a long-term rela-tionship, or something with formal parameters. Hell, I don't know. It's a fucking dream and it's stupid to question it.

I glide in and out of her, murmuring soothing nonsense like how hot she is, what a good girl she is to take my big dick so well. The words seem to get her off, because she's moaning louder, and I can feel the rhythmic tightening of her pussy as we fuck. She'll come soon, I bet, but I don't want this miracle dream to end.

I don't want to say goodbye to my new babydoll.

Then Ryder shows up. He's in front of her like magic, kneeling on the bed like I am, his cock out and pumping in and out of her mouth. He wraps her hair around his fist and uses it to guide her movements. Every thrust of his pushes her back on me.

"She's responsive," he says, a smile curling his lips.

"She loves punishment." I point to one of my handprints, which has reddened her ass cheek.

"You like to be punished, little girl?" Ryder asks, thrusting harder into her mouth. "If you've been bad, your daddies will hurt you, do you understand? And you might think you like it, but we'll make it hurt a lot."

Her pussy tightens on my cock. Fuck, she's like a piece of heaven, riding me in this dream.

I wake up when I come, and I'm alone in the darkness of my bedroom. Fuck. I haven't had a wet dream since I was a teenager.

And I haven't ached this bad for a woman since before Genevieve.

My nightstand clock tells me it's four in the morning. I don't have to be at Ironwood Security for several hours, but that's the life of a business owner—hours mean fuck-all when you're running the place. If I want to go in at four-thirty in the damn morning, I can go in at four-thirty. If I want to go in at eleven, and stay until nine in the evening, no one will question it.

Well, Ryder would tell me I need to get a fuckin' life, but that's nothing new.

I get into my shower to clean the jizz off my stomach, where most of it landed instead of on my sheets, thankfully. As streams of warm water flow over my head and drip over my back, I close my eyes and lose myself to the feeling of heat and contentment. My mind returns to the brown-haired woman from the dream. For some reason, I wish I'd gotten a better look at her face. All I caught was her profile when she took a breath while sucking off Ryder.

As my thoughts settle on her and her luscious, curvy ass, my contentment dissipates and turns into an all-consuming need. Before I know it, my dick is hard again. Unbelievable. I take it in my hand, stroke firmly, trying to recall the exact sound of Babydoll's voice while I plunged into her tight hole. In my mind, she moans just as loud and I reach around to run my fingers over her slippery clit. Her pussy's dripping with her arousal and she has to brace her hands on the wall of the shower to keep her balance.

I come again with a shout.

But by the time I'm all dried off and getting into my boxer briefs, the woman's sweet face—in profile, damn it, because I didn't see her straight on in my dream—floats into my head again, and my cock hardens.

Obviously it's time I go out and find a woman to hook up with. Even better if I can convince Ryder to join me. We can each show a woman a good time when we're on our own, but together, bringing a woman pleasure with our cocks and tongues? So much better.

Ryder

I wake up late, around seven-thirty. My cabin's quiet—it's why I picked this place next to the lake. So it isn't the city noise pollution that woke me up.

I flip over to my side, feel the drag of sheets over my dick. It's sensitive now, hard as a fuckin' log between my legs.

The threads of a dream are still lingering in my mind. It was a sex dream, and the only reason I didn't come was something woke me up. Dammit. There were the makings of a good dream, there.

My phone vibrates on the nightstand, and I realize that's what woke me. Fuck. I look down at my texts and see Jaxon has sent me a message. He probably wasn't worried about waking me up, because I'm usually wide awake by six.

Jaxon: *Club tonight?*

I fall back against the pillow and close my eyes. I don't want the club—I want the woman I was dreaming about. All I can recall is...shit, it's gone. I have the feeling of her warm mouth on my cock, and her tongue swirling up the length of it. A glimpse of mischief in her eyes, like she wants me to order her around so she can be a brat.

I love brats. I love to hear their sass, and then their moans when I spank the sass away.

Jaxon: *Don't ignore me, man. I'm not saying we have to marry the first girl we find. It can be casual.*

Flashes of my dream punch through my mind, each

one arousing me further. A casual night, sharing a woman's soft, welcoming, and enthusiastically consenting body with my best friend again...yeah. I could get on board with that.

Fuck yeah, I type back.

It's been way too long since we went after a girl together.

Jaxon

I walk into Club Vice. Not much has changed since I was last here, what, a year ago? Two? It's no surprise the place isn't just surviving, but thriving, because the owner, Margot, is a freaking business genius.

Ryder doesn't seem to be here yet, so I make my way through the crowd and find the last empty seat at the bar. They're in between DJ sets right now, so the music is muted and energy on the dance floor is low.

There are still people dancing, though. The lighting is low—no ridiculous flashing rave-like displays. Club Vice is understated, elegant. It's still a meat market, for sure, but it caters to people with a little more money than the average college student. We're not just looking to hook up, here; we're looking for an experience.

I order a drink and lean against the bar, waiting for Ryder. We usually like to check out available women together and decide who to try to pick up.

A man and woman sit on one side of me, close to the end of the bar. They're bickering loudly over the music, and I'm just about to wonder if the bouncer shouldn't come by and break the two of them up before the woman slams a beer bottle over the man's head or something—and then suddenly they're embracing and practically dry-humping at the bar.

Amused, I watch them for a minute, wondering just how far they're going to take this interlude. His hand is halfway up her dress, quite obviously stroking her pussy, and she's cupping his dick over his pants.

Someone shouts at them to get a room and they break apart, then quickly leave the club.

I finish my drink. As I set it down, I catch sight of two women sitting a few stools down from me—one has blond hair, and the other has dark red hair. The blond one leans back and I catch her friend in profile.

And there she is—it's her. The girl from my dream. Her hair's the wrong color, but that's her profile, exactly.

The word "babydoll" is on my lips already, but I keep it inside.

I flag down the bartender, who's been flirting with the girl's friend. I ask him to send over drinks with my compliments. He smiles at me knowingly. "I overheard the redhead just broke up with an asshole."

Rebound sex. It isn't my usual MO, but if she's happy about the break-up, maybe our time together could be more about celebration than revenge.

My babydoll looks over at me. Is she surprised I sent her a drink? She shouldn't be—she's so fucking gorgeous, it's a wonder she isn't surrounded by drinks sent to her by hopeful assholes like myself.

I debate going over to say hello. Ryder's nowhere in sight, but he'll get here soon. I should wait for him.

A few minutes later, the two women get up to dance.

I watch them for several long moments—and by "them" I mean "Babydoll," because I can't take my eyes off of her. A fierce, possessive feeling overtakes me. I have to make her mine, even if just for one night.

1

Olivia

When Samantha's text comes in, Daniel looks sharply at my phone, his green eyes narrowing. I don't know why it bothers him so much when I receive texts. He's more interested in the basketball game playing on my TV than he is in me.

"Who's texting you?" he asks.

"Samantha."

"Why?" His voice is belligerent, combative. He acts like it's weird for my own friend to text me.

"She wants to hang out." The words are out of my mouth before I've thought them through, and I immediately cringe. Daniel doesn't like Samantha. He hasn't liked any of my friends, actually, to the point that most of them have dropped off my radar—or rather, after I've said a hundred times that I can't hang out, they've stopped inviting me places.

Samantha is the one last hold-out.

"Well, tell her you can't," Daniel says, turning back to the TV. The glow of it reflects against his sandy brown hair—the product he puts in his hair makes it shiny. He continues, "You're hanging out with me tonight."

I look from him to the TV screen. Yeah, this is real quality time, me and my boyfriend of six months.

"Actually," I say, "let's see what she wants to do. Maybe we can all go somewhere."

He sticks his hand down the front of his sweatpants and scratches his nuts. Classy. "I'm comfy. We'll stay in. I'll take you out somewhere nice tomorrow night, promise."

Samantha texts a second time and my phone buzzes. *Hellooooo. You there?*

"Could she stop it with the texting already?" Daniel snaps.

I fumble with my phone, nearly dropping it in my haste to unlock it and write back to Samantha. Maybe if I'm fast enough, she'll get the hint.

I'll make another excuse. Like I always do. *Staying in tonight, sorry, not feeling great.* The lie pops into my head immediately, like I've been trained to spout it out. It's practically an earworm by this point, an old song I can't stop singing.

As my fingers hover over the keypad, though, I stop. Why should I stay here with Daniel McScratchyballs?

Why am I even *with* him?

It's almost as if I'm standing outside of my body, looking around at the scene. My living room, which used to be neat, has various piles stacked around it. Piles of Daniel's dirty clothes. Piles of his clean clothes. Piles of dishes he still hasn't taken to the kitchen after I flat-out refused to take them for him.

Beyond the physical evidence that this isn't working out, there's the tension in the air. My fear, mostly. Fear of him getting pissy and broody if someone texts me. Fear of spending an entire evening comforting him when he's butthurt over his team losing.

Fear of never getting out of this relationship.

Holy shit. Why haven't I broken up with this douchebag yet? Is it his looks? I used to find him attractive, and I suppose, objectively, he is, with his thick brown hair and green eyes. But nothing about him does it for me anymore. The only thing I feel when I look at him anymore is tension.

Clenching my phone in my hand, I say, "Daniel, we need to talk."

"What?" He keeps his gaze on the television screen.

"Dammit, Daniel, I'm trying to break up with you. Would you please pay attention?"

He sits up with a grunt and moves his feet to the floor. "Don't be stupid, Olivia. We're perfect together."

"This"—I wave my hands at my messy apartment, and then between him and me—"this is not perfect. This is not together. It's over."

"Wait a second. You don't want to do this without even talking to me first."

"This is me talking."

He shakes his head. "This is you having crazy time. Are you on the rag or something?"

"This is me finally seeing clearly everything that's going on here. Please leave my apartment. It's really over, and I'm not interested in talking things out."

"Olivia. Baby. I love you."

Six months and he never said those words until now. A week ago, I would've been thrilled at this little crumb that said our relationship was progressing right on track. Now, though, I see it as another way he's manipulating me.

Shaking my head, I say, "I'm going out with Samantha. When I get back here, you better be gone."

He stands up and moves toward me, but I whirl around. I grab my purse and I'm out the door, into the hallway. When I close the door to lock it after me, he's standing there, staring. He reaches down wordlessly and scratches his nuts again.

~

Olivia

I take the shot Samantha holds out, then lift it in a salute at the tall, commanding man sitting down the bar from us. He looks too sophisticated for a place like this, too handsome to be legal.

The crowded dance club is teeming with hundreds of people. Most of the women are dressed far sexier than me. Yet he's still looking at me.

Those other women are probably far more single than I am, too.

I'm single, yes. Thankfully so. But I just broke up with Daniel two hours ago. I should be sadder about this, right? And I am sad. Tears even fill my eyes. But they are tears of relief, not regret. The only regret I have is not dumping his ass sooner.

"You doing okay, Olivia?" Samantha asks.

I run a finger underneath my eyes, making sure none of the moisture smears my make-up as I wipe it away. "I'm good."

She leans over and gives me a hug, then turns to face the bar. Flagging down the bartender, she says, "Another round of...whatever it is that the man down there sent us."

The bartender winks. "No problem, chica."

Samantha bats her eyelashes at him. She's a shameless flirt, especially with bartenders. Something about them just does it for her.

I don't know how to tell her how grateful I am that she texted me tonight. She'd said nothing about Daniel, but the texts had sparked an inner revolution. Now that I'm away from Daniel's influence, I can better see what a bad place I'd been in.

Not only did Samantha spark that inner revolution, she'd also squeezed me into one of her dresses and done my make-up. She is incredible. As if sensing my feelings, she reaches over and squeezes my hand.

"You're the best," I tell her.

"I know," she says simply. "Now, tell me about your final project."

My final art project is a ginormous sculpture, but I haven't shown it to her yet. "It's a big, phallic monstrosity," I say.

She laughs. "It is not."

"I can't wait for you to see it," I say. "It's nearly finished."

"I keep trying to invite myself to your studio..."

"Soon," I say. "I promise."

I risk a peek back down the length of the bar. The man is still sitting there, but he isn't looking at me anymore.

I tell myself I'm not disappointed. My sheets probably still smell like Daniel—strong cologne that can't mask the stench of dirty feet.

"There aren't any cameras around, right?" I ask.

"Olivia. Seriously. No one is paying attention to you. My wig idea was genius, I will not-so-humbly admit, and your make-up makes you unrecognizable. Okay?"

"Okay." I touch one of my eyebrows. Samantha colored them with auburn eyeliner to match the wig, giving my natural medium brown hair and brows a little pop of color.

"Stop touching your face or you'll ruin your makeup," she says, grabbing my wrist.

The bartender brings over our shots and we tap the counter before tossing them back.

"Let's dance," Samantha says, jumping from her stool to do a little shimmy.

A pulsing beat has filled the club. Samantha and I aren't the only two heading out to the floor. Everything is loose and free. Those two shots were exactly what I needed. I resolve to forget the hottie who was parked a few seats down the bar from us, and I lose myself in dancing, instead.

My hips sway with the beat, my feet move, my body twirls. The press of people is sexy, intoxicating as the music. Strong hands grip my waist from behind, moving with my swaying for a few beats before taking control. I can't see the man who holds me, but his hands are warm and they caress my body even while they direct my movements.

Desire pools in my belly. I love being controlled like this—I always have. I used to want Daniel to take more control in the bedroom, but the one time I worked up the nerve to ask, he laughed at me.

When my cheeks heat at the memory, I start to lose the beat of the music. As if sensing my inattention, the man dancing with me yanks me back against him. My body is flush against his, and I feel his package nestled against my ass. The pounding music swallows my gasp.

He smells like citrus and leather. I try to turn, to see his face, but his grip keeps me in place. For some reason, I'm not bothered by this. Samantha is nearby, dancing in a group with some other women and men—including the bartender, who must be done with his shift or on a break. When I catch her attention, her eyes widen and she gives me an approving smile.

My partner lifts one of his hands from my waist and waves to someone else. Then finally, *finally*, he spins me around and I can look up into his face. It's the man from the bar. He's tall, which I had already guessed based on where his cock rested against my upper ass. What I hadn't known was just how handsome he would be. His cheekbones are prominent over a carefully trimmed beard. I can't see the color of his eyes in the dim club, but I can tell they're dark, and heavy-lidded. Bedroom eyes. His hair is dark, also, and cut short.

He takes my hands in his and links them around the back of his neck. It causes my body to move closer to him, and my braless chest mashes against his.

When a second set of hands grabs my waist, I jerk

forward into my dance partner. He bends slightly and whispers, "Easy. It's a friend of mine."

I turn my head to see his friend, but all I can glimpse is shaggy dark hair and blazing eyes, either a pale blue or green—I can't tell in the club's lighting.

Sandwiched between two guys—wow. I never would have imagined this at the start of my night. I look for Samantha again, and she's watching me with her mouth wide open.

"Get it, girl!" she calls, her words nearly drowned out by the music.

So I let the men manipulate me, bending my body to their will through that song, and the next. Every slide of hands, every press of their pelvises, every breath against my neck, and I grow more and more feverish with desire. I haven't ever felt so heavy, so ripe and ready.

The guy in front rubs his cheek against mine, his beard abrasive in a way that makes me shiver. The guy behind presses an open-mouthed kiss to the place where my neck meets my shoulder. Liquid desire spirals through my core. My moan is lost in the music, but he must sense it because he tightens his hands on my hips and yanks me against him. His cock is hard, and I rub my ass against him.

Wanton. Lustful. Horny.

The first guy reaches down and touches the place where my hem meets my thighs. He teases the skin there, fingers splaying upward beneath my skirt.

I hardly know myself. I'm ready to fuck two strangers on the dance floor.

2
____

Olivia

I wonder if it would be too forward of me to suggest we get a room at the hotel one block over. The very idea of speaking what I want causes my stomach to tie itself in knots. I've never been good about taking control. But I want to go somewhere with one of these guys, fuck out all the desire pounding through my core. My pussy has never felt so empty and needy. Surely one of them would say yes? If not both?

I nearly laugh at the thought. Inviting one of them for no-holds-barred sex is one fantasy entirely. Inviting two? I can't even comprehend it.

Then I feel the brush of skin on my inner thigh. My dress has been hiked up slightly in the front, but the guy there is blocking anyone's view.

A voice in my ear asks, "Is this okay?"

And the hand creeps upward. Hot. Confident.

I nod, but I can't believe what I'm about to say. Still, I want this—I want it more than anything. "Yes."

He reaches my folds, which are covered by a flimsy bit of lace, and he pushes my panties aside.

Holy fuck. We're really doing this. I look at the people dancing around us. They don't look our way, absorbed in their own dancing. Then I send my gaze up to the guy in front of me. His focus is intent on where the other guy's hand disappears beneath my skirt.

The second guy's finger slides along my already-wet pussy, and I whimper.

"Fuck," the guy in front of me says, flicking his gaze up to mine.

Music pulses around us, its beat heady and hypnotic. The guy behind me is rubbing against my ass while he fucks me with his fingers. My legs are weak and I hold tight to the arms of the man in front of me. Taken away by the sensation of my impending orgasm, I close my eyes.

The man in front leans close; I can feel his breath on my cheek. "Open your eyes, Babydoll."

One word, *babydoll*, not two. Somehow, I can see the letters in my mind, and they imprint there. I open my eyes, see his gaze clashing against mine. He brings up a hand and wraps it securely around my throat. Not a choke, but tight enough to hold my head in place as he lowers his lips to my mouth.

Citrus explodes over my tongue, and fire. He presses his tongue between my lips—commanding, claiming. I allow him in, kissing him back as if he's the very air I need to breathe.

I'm kissing one man while another one pumps a

second finger into my pussy. The heel of his hand rubs against my clit.

I come undone, crying out against the kiss.

They hold me in their arms, and we sway to the music as my aftershocks fade. I want more with them both. Right now. Here, in public, I don't care.

"Good job, Babydoll," the man in front of me says, then kisses my cheek.

The current song ends, and the guy behind me steps away. I crane my neck to look for him, but the guy in front of me touches my chin with a single finger and redirects my gaze toward his.

"I like eye contact," he reminds me in a deep voice that sends ripples of pleasure throughout me.

I'm careful to keep my gaze on his face.

"Good girl," he says.

Another ripple of pleasure, this one more like a wave, cascades within my body. My lips part and I want to kiss him so, so badly. I risk a glance at his mouth. His lips look soft yet firm against his beard. I already know they feel like heaven against my lips, and I want that again.

"Ah, I'd ruin you, Babydoll," he says.

Blinking up at him, I surprise myself when I say, "Maybe I'd like that."

He laughs—the bastard laughs. For some reason, that hurts more than anything else he could have done.

He adds, "You're so cute when you don't know what you're talking about."

Well, that's enough humiliation for one night. Daniel laughed at me—more than once. He always made me feel stupid. I don't need to stay here and let this total stranger make me feel stupid. I step back and look for Samantha.

"Come here, Babydoll," he says, gripping my wrist so I can't walk away.

I shoot him a look that I hope is laden with a combination of disgust and indifference. "My boyfriend is waiting for me."

"Don't insult me with an excuse like that," he says. "I'm sorry for laughing—trust me, it's nothing you did wrong."

Giving him a grumpy look, I pull away from his grasp and fold my arms over my chest.

He smirks. "Be a good girl and take this."

I watch as he pulls a card from his breast pocket, as well as a pen. He scribbles something on the back of the card and hands it to me.

His gaze intent on mine, he says, "If you're ever looking to get ruined—truly ruined—give me a call."

I will never call him. I take the card anyway, vowing to drop it on the floor as soon as he steps away.

But when he leaves, I tuck it into the top of my dress, where the tight fabric holds it in place.

3

Jaxon

It's with regret that I leave her on the dance floor. Ryder took off too fast, but I get it—he doesn't want to get involved.

Still, I can't help but think he acted like a dick. We just danced with the most exquisite woman I've ever laid eyes on, and he takes off immediately after making her come all over his fingers?

I can just imagine him now. *You get too attached, too fast, Jaxon. Remember Genevieve.*

Yeah, I fucking remember Genevieve.

The bouncer waves at me as I leave the club. No, I don't own the place, what kind of cliché do you think I am? But I do come here frequently enough to know some of the staff.

Cool night air caresses my face. I remember her lips on mine. My cock is thick and heavy. If I'd been standing behind her like Ryder was, I'd have been fucking her in the middle of all those people, no question. And I'd have been fucking her with my cock, not my fingers.

Pulling my phone from my pocket, I call Ryder.

"What?" he says by way of answering.

Rude motherfucker. "You took off rather fast from the club."

"Yeah, well, places to go, work to do."

The sounds of traffic come through my phone; he's talking to me through his speakers while he drives.

"We could have brought her to my place, shown her a good time," I say.

"Nope."

I take the phone from my ear to glare at the screen, as if that will do any good. "What did you just say?"

"I just said *nope*, and I think you fuckin' heard me, asshole."

What the hell? "What got into you?" I ask, all friendliness gone from my voice.

"You know."

"No, I honestly don't. Please, enlighten me, if you can take a few moments from your busy schedule."

Sarcasm isn't the way we usually talk to each other, but he's being a dick.

"You called her *babydoll*," he snarls.

"Ah."

"Yeah, *ah*. It starts with a pet name and then you're keeping her and falling in love and then it's like Genevieve all over again."

Called it. I look to the night sky, which is blank of stars from the light pollution, and I'm searching for some kind of neon light declaring that I'm a winner. I knew Ryder was going to bring up Genevieve.

The valet brings my car around, and I pass him a tip that makes him stutter, "Thank you," over and over.

I wave at him, climb in the car, and say into my phone, "Just because I gave her a pet name doesn't mean she's Genevieve. Hell, Ryder, I think that woman wrecked you more than she wrecked me, and I was fucking engaged to her."

Silence on the other end of the line.

"Ryder?" I say.

"Gotta go."

The call ends.

Ryder and I have been best friends since college—sharing a dorm room, then an apartment, and now a business. Throughout it all, we found that we were also very good at sharing women. It works for our dominant, kinky sides, and so far, all of our playmates have been more than pleased.

Even Genevieve was pleased, for quite a long time. Until things went sour.

I want to tell Ryder that I think this woman from the club could be different, that if she calls me, I'll drop everything to ruin her as I promised. But that would mean telling him that I gave her my number, and he'll be pissed about that, too.

I hope he gets over it, because it's been far too long since we entertained a woman in bed for more than a weekend. I'm ready for something lasting, something real.

And my palm itches when I think about reddening that babydoll's fine ass.

～

Ryder

I tear up the road in my haste to get out of the city. Gotta put more distance between me and Jaxon and the girl.

The girl especially. She smelled like fucking candy. So sweet, so hot. I only knew one other woman who could embody sexy and sweet so wholly before.

Jaxon's right—Genevieve ruined me. I'm still not over her and I doubt I ever will be, and that's fine. It's easy enough to find a willing woman to join us every now and then. I try to lose myself in recalling our last partner. She was deliciously curvy. I loved the way her ass moved when I smacked it, and her tits had been magnificent, overfilling my palms while I leaned over her from the back and stroked into her ass. She'd been hypersensitive to nipple play, which had been fucking fun.

I wonder how sensitive Babydoll's nipples are. It's too bad I didn't get a chance to touch them, see how much more she'd grind against my cock. Would she say it's too much and try to squirm away? Or would she arch into my pinching attention?

Fuck, how did this turn into a fantasy about the girl from the club? I try to redirect my imagination to the last woman, but as I try to picture her mouth on my cock, it's instead the girl from the club, Jaxon's new babydoll, whose lips I see. It's her tight pussy I smell on my fingers right now. I should've washed my hand, but like a sick motherfucker, I wanted to carry her candy scent a little longer.

I'll clean it away as soon as I get to my cabin retreat.

4

———

Olivia

"Bye!" I wave to Samantha and her new bartender boy toy in the back seat of the Lyft as they drive off. Then I punch in the door code and enter my building. The doorman is on a break, so I scurry to the elevator and make my way to my floor. The key to my apartment is already in my hand.

For the first time, I'll be going into an empty apartment. I'm buzzed enough to give myself a literal pat on the back as I make my way down the hall. It certainly hadn't been easy telling Daniel to pack up his few things and leave tonight, but I'd done it. I'd stuck up for myself.

And I'd nearly thrown up afterward. Damn, I hated being an adult. Confrontation was the worst.

When I jab my key into the lock, it doesn't turn. Annoying. I try again, reorienting the key.

It still doesn't work.

I look up and down the hall. Am I more than buzzed?

Am I drunk? So drunk that I'm trying to open someone else's apartment door? But a glance at the number in front of me confirms this is my place.

I try one more time.

"Fuck," I mutter. In my irritation, I bang my hand against the wall.

The door across from my apartment opens, and my neighbor Seth sticks his bearded face out. "Hey, Olivia. Wow, great wig."

I touch the auburn wig covering my hair, surprised. I'd forgotten I was wearing it.

Guilt settles in my chest, though—Seth battles with insomnia. I shouldn't have been so loud. "I'm so sorry if I woke you."

"Nah, I'm binge-watching a nature documentary." He holds up a mug of tea that smells strongly of chamomile. "But look, the guy came to change your locks an hour ago. Maybe try your new key?"

I mouth the words. Changed my locks. Try a new key.

"Motherfucker!" I yell at my door.

"Whoa, Olivia," Seth says.

"Daniel changed my locks." Squeezing my eyes shut, I try to take a breath, but all I can do is mutter, "Fuck. *Fuck.*"

I reach into my purse for my phone. I'll call Samantha and stay with her while I figure out my next move.

The phone's dead. I choke back a sob. This is fine. I'll figure it out.

Seth is watching me, a concerned expression on his face. "Is there anything I can do? I mean, you can't stay here because my mom will flip, but...anything else?"

Seth lives with his mother, who, despite having been

told numerous times that her son is gay, believes that he's going to marry me and give her several grandchildren.

I sigh. This sucks on so many levels. "Do you have a charger I can borrow?"

He looks at my phone. "Not one that would match that. I only have a landline. You can call whoever you want from it, though. Just keep quiet so you don't wake my mom."

I have exactly zero phone numbers memorized. Zero. Who remembers phone numbers anymore? Not this girl. People used to write them down, back in the day. Sometimes they'd hand them out on business cards—

Wait.

There's one phone number.

Seth's eyes get big as I run a finger down the top of my dress and pull out the gray card the guy handed me in the club.

Jaxon Marsel, it reads. There's no number on the front, but on the back, I see his handwriting. Bold, no-nonsense. I bet he's the kind of guy who always writes in all-caps.

I also bet he's the kind of guy who can tell me what to do. He'll have a plan for how I should resolve this issue.

He's also the only contact I have.

"Someone gave you their card?" Seth says. "That's old-school. And soooo sexy. Are they hot?"

"He is, yeah," I say.

"Come in, give him a call." Seth beams. "Maybe I'll make popcorn and watch."

I roll my eyes and go into his apartment. I follow him to an ancient rotary phone nestled beneath a pile of papers on the counter. I knew Seth and his mom don't get out much, but damn.

"Does this thing even work?" I ask.

He laughs quietly. "Yep. Do you think you know how to use it?"

"I've seen old movies, sure I know." It only takes me three tries to get the number dialed.

A gruff voice answers immediately. "Jaxon here."

I'm suddenly tongue-tied. "Um..."

"Spit it out, sweetheart, it's two a.m."

I can hear that he's moving around, maybe walking through his apartment. Ha. He doesn't have any old apartment, I'm sure. He has some swanky penthouse in the nicest part of San Esteban.

"I'm sorry to call you," I say. "I just don't know who else to call, and...we met at the club tonight?"

The sounds of movement on the other end of the line stop. "What happened?"

"We...we danced. With your friend."

"No." He gives a little laugh. "I remember that. I mean, what's wrong now? If you're in danger, you should be calling the police, not me."

"This is more of a personal matter," I say, looking over at Seth.

Seth nods and waves at me to continue. Jaxon's silent, waiting for my explanation.

I say, "My ex has locked me out of my apartment. I was hoping for advice, I guess."

"Give me your address."

"I don't know—"

His voice is a growl. "Do you want my help or not, princess?"

In a quiet voice, I recite the address.

"Are you in a safe place?" he asks.

"Yes, I'm in a friend's apartment, but I can't stay here."

As if on cue, Seth's mom calls out, "Seth, darling? Is that the television? Turn it down, please."

"Sure, Mom," he shouts back. To me, he says, "Olivia, sorry, but you gotta go."

"Right."

"Meet me in the lobby," Jaxon says. "*Inside.* I'll be there in ten minutes."

"Got it," I say quietly. "See you soon."

I hang up the phone and stare wide-eyed at Seth. "He's coming here. To get me."

"Seth?" his mom shouts again.

"Shoo," Seth says to me. "Go get your business card hottie. Have wild, kinky sex. Then tell me all about it tomorrow."

I shake my head at him and gather my purse with the dead phone. Maybe Jaxon will have a charger I can use. Just wait until Samantha hears what Daniel did. She'll make immediate plans for eviscerating him.

Before I go, I leave the business card with Seth. It seems safer for some reason. Not that I'm afraid; I just don't want to be totally stupid.

"Thank you," I whisper to Seth, and then head downstairs.

Down in the lobby, everything is quiet. Eerily quiet. The doorman still isn't back from his break, and maybe he fell asleep somewhere. My mother wouldn't be happy to find out that this place's security isn't as legit as she'd wanted; as a congresswoman, she's been very involved in my living situation, opting to supplement the cost of renting an apartment if the security is better.

The lobby is starting to give me the creeps. The sidewalk beyond the big windows is crowded, people bustling around as they usually would on a Saturday night.

Needing the cool outside air and the noise of other humans, I step through the lobby doors to wait for Jaxon.

A black sports car pulls up minutes later, and Jaxon climbs out from behind the wheel. His dark eyes survey me and an angry frown appears on his face.

"What are you doing out here?" he asks.

"I—I'm waiting for you."

He hurries over to me and takes my hand. "Did I or did I not ask you to wait *inside* the lobby?"

"Now that I recall," I say as he practically drags me to the car, "there was no *asking* about it. Who are you, my dad?"

"That's a lot funnier than you intend it to be," he says, a dark undertone of humor in his voice.

5

―――――――

Olivia

That makes no freaking sense, but whatever. He opens the passenger door and helps me into the seat.

"Are you going to buckle me up, since I'm so help-less?" I ask.

Immediately, my cheeks grow hot. I, a near stranger to him, am asking for his help in saving my ass from sleeping in my apartment building's hallway. Perhaps I should turn down the snark.

"Sorry," I start to say.

But he's already leaning over me and buckling my seatbelt. His face is close to mine as he does it, and I pull in his citrus and leather scent. This man is so gorgeous. I have no idea why he's helping me. I don't know what I'd expected, maybe that he'd have the number of an emergency locksmith, or know of a hotel where I could stay.

But instead, here he is, in the flesh, taking me...somewhere.

My mother would kill me. I'm getting in the car of a stranger. This was a terrible idea. At least I left Jaxon's card with Seth. It seems a flimsy safeguard, but it's something.

He seems to realize this as he gets behind the wheel, and he says, "You can call Detective Baldwin with San Esteban PD. He'll vouch for me. You could post a picture of us together on a social media channel, but that's likely to do more damage to your reputation than save you from something else."

No, no pictures on social media. Despite the fact I'm still in a wig and make-up, I'm not risking it.

"I'm good, thanks," I say.

"You're obviously not good," he says, handing me his phone. "Call your friend and let her know where you're going."

"I don't know her number."

He curses under his breath, and I can't help the sick feeling of shame growing in my gut.

"I'm sorry," I say. "I know I shouldn't have called you, but yours was the only number...I shouldn't have. I probably woke you up."

"You didn't wake me up, Babydoll," he says in a gentler voice.

I wrap my fingers around and around each other, needing the movement to focus on so I don't fall apart. "I just didn't know what to do."

Softly, he says, "And you called me, and I'm going to help you."

I exhale. This was exactly what I wanted—what I needed. Someone to take charge. It feels seven shades of messed up that I'm throwing myself at the nearest guy to solve my problems, but something about Jaxon makes me feel safe. What I did in the club with him and his friend? I never would've dreamed of that with anyone else. I knew they'd keep me safe and that no one would know what we were doing from the way they shielded my body as we danced.

We pull into a parking garage underneath a building and he parks the car.

"Stay put, and I'll help you out," he says before exiting.

Perfectly capable of leaving a vehicle, I unbuckle the seatbelt and grip the door handle.

He's there already, opening the door and frowning at me. "Babydoll, we need to have a discussion about a few things. Namely, if I tell you to do or not do something, you obey."

"Look, Jaxon, I appreciate the help, but it doesn't mean you get to be my boss."

He grins. "This is going to be fun. Come on, Babydoll."

"Wait a minute," I say, accepting his hand and allowing him to pull me from the car. "Why are you helping me, anyway? You could've told me to fuck off."

"I like you," he says simply.

I follow him to an elevator where he punches in a code. The doors open, we step in, and then we're enshrouded in silence. The walls are mirrored and I take in my appearance—my slinky dress from the club, a smudge of lipstick next to the corner of my mouth, the eyeliner much darker than I would normally wear it.

My head is starting to itch from the wig, and the band feels tight. "Who do I call when someone's squatting in my apartment?" I ask.

"The police."

"It's hardly an emergency."

He gives a little laugh. "You do know there's a non-emergency number, right?"

"Yeah," I say slowly. "I just didn't think...ugh, I feel so stupid."

"Nah, you've had a long night, several drinks, the orgasm of your life on the dance floor while sandwiched between two hot men"—he gives me a roguish wink—"and then you came home to whatever domestic dispute is going on. It's hard to make decisions when you're in a situation like that."

We step off the elevator and directly into a penthouse. I can see the city from wall-to-wall windows. This probably isn't the tallest building in San Esteban, but it's damn close. My mother was an attorney who later became a congresswoman, and I've always had enough money. I've attended fundraisers with her and rubbed elbows with aristocrats. But I've never been in an apartment this nice before, and I can't help but gawk. The décor is subtly rich, in grays and blues, with lighting that invites my gaze past the sitting area and to art on the few places of the wall that aren't taken up by floor-to-ceiling windows.

"Can I get you some water?" he asks.

I'm relieved he's not offering me alcohol. I don't think

my system could take any more tonight. "Yes, please. And can I use your restroom?"

"First door on the left," he says, pointing to a hallway.

I find the bathroom and am unsurprised to see that it's just as luxurious as the rest of the penthouse. Before I leave it, I pull the wig from my head. My brown hair beneath is smooshed down and kind of bonkers, but the relief of being rid of the wig is worth it. I find a hair elastic in my purse and put my locks up into a bun. The auburn wig doesn't fit in my purse, so I carry it out of the bathroom with me.

Jaxon turns when I emerge from the hallway, two bottles of water in his hands. His jaw drops when he sees me.

"Sorry," I say, "I know, my hair looks crazy."

"No, you just look different, that's all," he says. His dark gaze roves over my body, as if he's wondering what other secrets I'm hiding.

"I promise, my only disguise was the wig. My mother is in politics, so when I want to let loose, I try not to be recognized."

"Do you often want to let loose?" he asks, a strange expression on his face.

"Are you judging me?" I ask. "After you and your friend practically fucked me inside a crowded club?"

"No. Fuck no. Not judging." He holds up his hands, and the water in one of the bottles sloshes. He hands me the other one, which is still capped and sealed. He probably left it sealed so I'd feel more comfortable, and the thoughtfulness makes me soften somewhat.

"Thanks," I say, taking the water.

"I'm just curious about you, that's all. I still don't know your name, Babydoll."

I wink. "I like *Babydoll* just fine, but you can also call me Olivia."

"Olivia." He holds out a hand for me to shake. "I'm Jaxon."

"It's nice to meet you," I say.

He keeps hold of my hand and tugs me a little closer. "Tomorrow, we're going to call the police and figure out how to get your apartment back. Tonight, we should talk."

There's a heat in his eyes—the same heat I'd seen at the club, and I wonder what I've gotten myself into.

"What do you want to talk about?"

"Remember when I gave you my card?" he asks. "I told you to call me if you were looking to get ruined."

"I—this is an extenuating circumstance," I say.

The heat in his eyes fades and he lets go of my hand. "Okay. The second door on the left is the guest room and there's a bed made up already."

I frown up at him. I hadn't expected him to release me quite so easily. My disappointment settles over my shoulders like a heavy shawl. "Thank you."

"You're welcome, Babydoll."

When I turn around and walk to the guest room, I can feel his gaze on my back, and I can't help but put an extra swing in my step.

"You're playing with fire, Babydoll," he drawls, and I hurry to the bedroom without any more flouncing.

Inside, I find a pair of men's sweatpants and t-shirt that he must have gotten out for me to sleep in. I change into them, feeling more naked than before. My tiny club dress covered less skin, but wearing someone else's clothes is surprisingly intimate.

The clothes smell like citrus, but the bed smells like pine, and somehow the two scents work together to pull me into sleep as soon as I close my eyes.

6

Jaxon

At five a.m., I'm still awake. Olivia is sleeping just two rooms away, and every cell in my body yearns to go to her. Does she know she's mine yet? I want her so fucking bad, my dick hasn't calmed down since the club.

But I need to wait until she wants me back, and I don't think she's in that place yet.

Soft whimpering sounds reach my ears, and I sit up to listen better. Is Olivia crying? I'm tempted to go to her, but maybe I should give her space. She indicated that she's not here to let me ruin her. But comforting isn't the same as ruining. At least, it doesn't have to be.

My particular brand of comfort can definitely ruin a woman.

I can control myself, though. If she needs something —whatever it is—I'm going to offer it to her.

I don't want to waste time overthinking it; I go to the guest room. "Olivia?"

She's on her side, eyes closed. Her entire body is curled up tightly, as if she's hiding from something.

"Olivia," I say. "Olivia, you're having a nightmare."

She moans and jerks in her sleep.

"Babydoll, wake up," I say in a louder voice.

Gasping, she opens her eyes. Her body relaxes a fraction, but she remains tense overall.

"You okay?" I give in to the overwhelming desire to comfort her, sitting down on the bed and taking her hand.

"I had a dream that my ex was after me," she says, still breathing hard.

"Is he abusive?" I ask. A primal part of me is already getting dressed, grabbing a baseball bat, and running to her old apartment to kick his ass.

"Not at all, he's just a douche," she says. "Sorry for waking you."

"It's all right," I say. "Do you want me to wait here, Babydoll?"

"Hmm? No, I'll be okay."

I chuckle. "Then you might want to let go of my hand."

She sits up a little and sees where our hands are joined. "Oh, sorry."

But she doesn't let me go.

"I'll stay here, if you want," I say.

She glances quickly at me in the dim light before looking away. "I'd like that."

"Okay." Lying down on top of the sheets next to her, I inhale her sweet scent. Fuck, she even smells like a babydoll, sweetness and candy. I wonder if she likes lollipops, and the thought of her lips closing over candy has my cock back to its rock-hard state.

I try to breathe evenly and eventually calm myself down. Then Olivia scoots closer to me and lays her head on my shoulder.

"Is this okay?" she asks.

"Yes." Inwardly, I'm grumbling. I should be the one asking consent for things. She's already turning me upside down.

Ryder would be furious, and for some reason, that idea makes me smile. Wait until he finds out the woman he finger-fucked in the club is sleeping in the guest room where he usually sleeps when he's in town.

Once Olivia's breathing becomes deep and even, I allow myself to close my eyes. Finally, I fall asleep.

I WAKE up lying on my side, a warm breast cupped in my hand and a plump little bottom pressed against my dick. Absently, I rub my boner in the crease of the woman's ass and caress the breast in my palm. My bed partner moans softly and presses her ass harder against my cock.

Yeah, I'm ready to go. I pinch her nipple and listen to her soft gasp before I bring my hand down to her waist.

The sweatpants she's wearing surprise me, because my female partners usually sleep naked or in the cute little nightgowns I buy for them. In the brief moment it takes me to realize this, I wake up fully.

It's Olivia in front of me, the woman I met last night. Her messy bun of brown hair spills across the pillow next to mine, and she's wearing my t-shirt and a pair of my sweats. Her skin seems to glow in the late morning light peeking through the dark curtains. I want to kiss the place on her neck right beneath her ear.

But we haven't talked about doing anything like this. Reluctantly, I let go of her breast and flip over on my back.

"Jaxon?" she asks, spinning around. "I need you."

Words that would normally crush my resolve into dust. "We haven't talked about how this usually goes," I say.

"So you're kinky, I get it," she says. "You want to spank me or something?"

I can't help it, I laugh.

She sits up slightly, bracing her arms on my chest. The indignation on her face is priceless as she says, "You don't have to make fun of me."

"Not making fun of you, Babydoll," I say. "What I want isn't the kind of thing you'd read in a bored house-wife's erotic fiction collection."

Wrinkling her nose, she sits all the way up on her knees and stares down at me. A faint blush covers her cheeks and moves down to her neck. "Then what is it you want?"

"I do like giving spankings, to naughty girls who deserve them. But I also like rewarding good little girls who listen to their daddies."

She thinks about that for a moment, and I love the way her forehead wrinkles while she does. "I've heard of this," she finally says. "So you're a daddy dom?"

I shrug. "If you have to put a label on it, yeah, I suppose I am."

I love that she isn't immediately dismissing the idea. It gives me hope that she might be into it.

She considers me with her gray eyes, and her plump lips are slightly pursed.

After a long moment, I ask, "Does some part of this appeal to you?"

"I guess it depends." Her eyes are wide, guileless. "I mean, I don't know much about it."

"That's okay. There's a lot of ways that people do age play. Some parts of it appeal to me—greatly—and other parts don't appeal in the slightest. We could find out what you like, if anything."

She's turned on—I can tell from the way she squirms slightly, as if she's trying to relieve an emptiness in her pussy.

"Is there something you need, Babydoll?" I ask.

"I already told you," she whispers.

"It might be good to tell me again."

"I need you."

"Do you want to try this like I want to do it, or do you want something vanilla?"

She freezes, like she wasn't expecting to make a decision. And that's when I know my babydoll was made for me. She wants cock, but she doesn't want to say how she gets it.

"You're waiting for me to take control," I say.

Nodding, she looks away.

"Eye contact, please," I remind her.

She snaps her gaze back to mine. The soft gray of her eyes reminds me of the ocean on a cloudy day.

"If you feel uncomfortable at any time," I say, "you can use a safe word and everything stops. Your safe word should be something weird, that someone wouldn't usually say during sex."

"Like...*bananas*?"

I nod and smile to show her I'm pleased. "That's a good safe word. Is that what you want to have as yours?"

"Hmm, no. I think I'd like mine to be *ponies*."

"Sounds good." I sit up and give her my first order. "Off the bed."

"What? Why?"

"Because I will spank your bottom if you don't do as I say."

She hurries off the bed and stands next to it.

"That nightstand, there. Open the drawer."

She does as I ask, and I enjoy the way her lips part in surprise at the sight of everything stored in there. Lube, condoms, and nipple clamps, if I'm remembering correctly from the last time Ryder and I entertained a woman in this room. Maybe some candy and soft black rope. I wonder if Olivia will like being restrained. I wonder if she'll like spankings. I sure hope so—I can't wait to put my handprints on her ass.

"Take out a condom and put it on my cock," I say, moving to the edge of the bed and planting my feet on the floor.

Her eyes widen, but she hurries to obey.

"Good girl," I say as she opens the foil packet.

I push my pants down enough to reveal my dick, and she rolls the condom over it. Her touch on me is soft and tentative.

"Are you nervous, Babydoll?" I ask.

She shakes her head.

I grab her chin in my hand and look her in the eyes. "Be honest with me. Every time. Are you nervous?"

"A little," she admits.

"Talk to me. Tell me why."

This obviously makes her uncomfortable. I wonder what her sex life was like before, if she isn't used to communicating about her feelings when things start getting intense. It'll be an interesting challenge, teaching her how to discuss her needs and wants.

"I'm worried about disappointing you," she says.

I move my hand from her chin to her neck and bring her head down to mine. After pressing a soft kiss against her mouth, I lean back and whisper, "You have nothing to worry about, then. I'm not going to be disappointed."

"Okay." She nods.

"Now climb onto my lap, Babydoll, and take my cock in your pussy."

7

———————

Olivia

At first I can only stare at Jaxon. Just like that? Sit on his cock?

It's a gorgeous cock, though. I certainly won't mind sitting on it. I've been thinking about doing just that since I woke up to the feeling of it pressed against my ass.

This is crazy. I just met this guy.

"I'm not a patient man, Babydoll."

"Right. Okay."

I start to pull off the t-shirt I'm wearing, but he says, "Leave that on. Just take off the sweats."

"Okay." I slip them off. "Underwear, too?"

"Show me."

The dark timbre of his voice alone could make me wet. I slowly lift the bottom of the shirt up to reveal my plain white thong—the pair of undies I'd had on when I left the apartment after breaking up with Daniel.

"Nice," he says, his dark brown eyes growing darker. "Now take off the panties and get on my dick before I lose my patience."

I quickly slip off the thong and step toward him. This feels awkward, all of a sudden, but I'm committed now. I really, *really* want this. My breasts feel heavy and full, my pussy is slick with need.

His pants aren't all the way down, just far enough that his cock can stick out. I slide over his knees and into his lap.

"Olivia, Babydoll," he says, kissing my cheek. "That's good. Now sit all the way down, and take my cock like a good girl."

Wow, so dirty. Yet I love it. I lower myself down slightly until I can feel his tip at my entrance. He's big, but I'm wet enough. He holds his cock in place and I lower again, my thighs straining.

He's in. Not all the way, just the tip. I can tell this isn't going to be an easy fit, but that's okay.

"You doing all right?" Jaxon asks.

"Mm-hmm."

"Can I help you?"

"Yeah," I say.

He wraps his arms around me. They're strong bands holding me in place, and he slowly lowers me the rest of the way onto his cock. My mouth falls open at the feeling of him inside of me. So big, so hard. My pussy stretches to accommodate him, and I feel him *everywhere*.

"Doing okay?" he asks.

"Yeah. It'll be better once we start moving." I begin to lift off of him.

His arms are tight, so tight I can't lift myself up. "Did I

forget to tell you, Babydoll? I just want you to sit here. I don't want you to move."

"I—what? No, you didn't say that. Why?"

I *need* to move. Holding him inside of me like this is torture. My body demands the friction of him moving within, and I'm craving the way I know our pleasure would heighten with the speed of his thrusts. I know how this dance is supposed to go; I've done it countless times with a few different partners.

So why does Jaxon want me to be still?

He keeps me in place and kisses my mouth. The slide of his tongue across my lips is slick, sensuous. I kiss him back, moaning. The need to move is all-encompassing. I can't lift off of his cock to get the friction I so desperately desire, so I wiggle a little from side to side.

"Oh, Babydoll. Don't make me punish you." He smiles, as if he really does want to punish me.

Of course he does.

"Are you a sadist?" I ask.

His smile grows even larger. "Maybe a little."

Annoyed, I resolve not to give him an excuse to punish me. I'll deny him that pleasure because he's denying me the pleasure of bouncing on his dick like I really want to do.

"Oh, so you're a stubborn one," he says, sliding his bearded cheek against mine to whisper in my ear. "I like that."

I give a little huff of exasperation, but it turns into a moan when I feel his cock twitch inside of me.

Ignoring my sounds, he says, "This is called cock-warming. I'll ask you to do this from time to time, because I like the feel of your tight little pussy hugging my cock. If I say, 'Babydoll, warm Daddy's cock,' you'll know what I'm talking about, won't you?"

"Daddy?" I ask.

"Yes, Babydoll?"

That wasn't what I meant. I'd meant the whole *daddy* thing was unexpected, despite having heard the phrase *daddy dom* before. But now I'm starting to get it. Age play. Babydoll. Spankings. Calling him *daddy* goes right along with that.

And I have to admit, the idea isn't repulsive. I wouldn't have thought I'd be into this sort of thing, but it's working for me. I mean, obviously it's working, if I'm sitting in his lap and warming his cock.

But the sensation of him inside of me, not moving, is driving me mad with need.

"I need to move on you," I say.

"You can wait," he says simply.

"No, I really need it."

He grins and kisses my cheek. "I might have something for you, so hang on a sec."

I frown. I'm not going anywhere.

When he reaches toward the open nightstand drawer, it causes our bodies to move slightly. I try to take advantage and wiggle a little more, but he draws his hand back from the nightstand, reaches for my breast, and pinches my nipple through the t-shirt—hard.

"Ow!" I yelp.

"Do *not* move," he says.

I can't help the whimper that comes from my throat. "Okay."

This time when he goes for the drawer, I bite my lip and try to stay still.

He comes back with a piece of candy. "Do you like butterscotch?"

"It's all right," I say.

"Okay. This is a hard candy. You can suck on it, but not chew it. Once it's gone, you can stop warming my cock and I'll give you what you need. Understand?"

"Yes." I nod.

"Yes, *Daddy*."

"Yes, Daddy."

"Good girl." He unwraps the butterscotch and waits until I part my lips, then he slides it into my mouth.

Sugary sweetness coats my tongue. He watches me suck on the candy, then kisses my mouth again. He sweeps his tongue across my lips, then inside. Now we both taste like butterscotch.

Lust gathers where we join, demanding that I rub against him. If I feel the slightest movement against my clit right now, I think I'll come immediately. He wouldn't even have to do any work. Infuriating man.

"You okay, Babydoll?"

"I wish you would just let me come," I say, my voice a whimper.

The candy is about half the size it was. I think of swallowing it and telling him that it got sucked away, but I also have a feeling that somehow, he would know exactly what I'd done.

"Show me your tongue," he says.

I stick it out, cupping the candy in it.

"Good job." Keeping his arms banded around my back, he gives two short thrusts into my pussy.

"Oh fuck," I gasp. So close. So very close.

He stops moving and kisses my lips.

"What did you do that for?" I ask, pouting at him.

"Ah, Olivia. I couldn't resist. Are you done with your candy yet?"

I suck on it furiously, trying to get it down to nothing. When it's just a sliver on my tongue, I show it to him again. He kisses me hard, sucking it into his mouth. Then he lets go of me and lies back on the bed.

"What are you doing?" I ask.

"You finished your candy, Babydoll. Now you can do what you want."

"I want your shirt off," I say.

He pulls it up and over his head, revealing a set of sculpted abs and a wide, hard chest with a subtle sprinkling of hair across it. A fainter trail of hair leads down from his navel to his cock.

I can now see exactly where we join, and every part of me throbs with need and want. I shift up and down experimentally. Sparks of desire shoot throughout my body. Closing my eyes, I move again, a little faster.

"Eye contact, Babydoll," Jaxon says. "Daddy wants to see your eyes when you come."

Oh my gosh, his words. So dirty. I open my eyes, staring directly into his.

All I need is a touch on my clit, and I'll be done. I want to savor the moment, but the whole cock-warming thing got me more than ready and I'm about to explode.

When I start to reach for my clit, Jaxon grabs my hand. "You're ready to come? That's my job."

"Please," I say, fighting against his grasp.

"Oh, Babydoll," he says, holding me tighter. With his other hand, he moves toward my clit. I lift up and down, taking him in and out of me, and he begins to meet me, thrusting in time to my movements.

When he touches my clit, I shatter.

Before I have a chance to recover, he flips us over and begins to stroke furiously within me, powerful thrusts that shake the entire bed. He lifts up the t-shirt I'm wearing and palms my breasts, squeezing the nipples between his fingers. If he were someone else, I might think the pinching was accidental, but I'm starting to understand Jaxon. He wants to dominate me thoroughly.

And I want to let him.

Another orgasm builds he continues to fuck me. I grab his shoulders, hanging on tight because this climax just might be the end of me—it grows more and more powerful and electric, like my nerve endings are going to fry.

"Come again for me, Babydoll," he says. "Eyes on me."

The words, his tone, the steely, dominating look in his deep brown eyes, the thrusting of his cock, the pinch on my nipples—all of it comes together to throw me over the edge of expectation and into ecstasy.

I cry out and he kisses me hard, muffling my cries with his mouth. His eyes never leave mine, and then he tenses up, going still inside me except for the telltale twitching of his cock as he comes.

8

Jaxon

I don't want to let go of her. Her body is languid, pliant beneath mine, and she smells sweet like butterscotch. I want to crawl down her body and taste her pussy until she's begging me for release again, but we have work to do.

"So your ex is squatting in your apartment?" I say, rolling off of her and removing the condom. I go into the attached bathroom and dispose of the rubber, then return to the guest room.

"That's my guess," she says. "I don't know why else he'd change the locks."

"Just to spite you," I say, "although I don't know him, so I can't guess what he'd do."

She slides off the bed and bends down to pick up her thong, then grimaces.

"Panties too wet to put back on?" I ask.

"Yeah." She shrugs and starts to step into them anyway.

"Go without," I say.

I fucking love the way her gray eyes widen and a blush tinges her cheeks when I surprise her like that. It makes me want to keep doing it.

"Do you want to tell me what to wear, too?" she asks in a snotty voice.

Oh, I need to have words with her. Advancing toward her, I make my voice low and controlled. "Lose the attitude, Babydoll. And listen closely."

She gasps when I press her up against the wall, holding her in place with my hips. My dick is already semi hard again, just from dominating her like this. Fuck, I want nothing more than to hole up in this guest room for two weeks and really show her what it would mean to be my babydoll.

As soon as we resolve this issue with her squatter ex, that's exactly what we'll do.

"Are you listening?" I ask.

"Yes," she whispers.

"Yes, what?"

She makes a soft little whimper. "Yes, Daddy."

"Good girl. You should feel free to act the brat with me all you want, but when you do, you should expect punishment. And if you think punishment sounds fun, then you haven't seen my particular brand of punishment. It's filthy and painful. Remember what I said last night, about what would happen if you called me?"

"That...that you'd ruin me."

I nod. "That's right."

Her breathing is rapid, her breasts nearly touching

my chest. Snaking one hand up under her t-shirt, I find her breast and lightly pinch the nipple.

She gasps and closes her eyes. "Yes."

Then I pinch harder.

Her eyes snap open, big gray oceans. She blinks back tears and says, "Ow, ow, ow."

I don't let go, wanting to help her get my point. Instead, I watch her carefully, waiting to see when the pain morphs into pleasure.

It happens quickly, which pleases me greatly. She begins to squirm.

When I let her go, she moves forward, following my hand, as if asking for more punishment to her nipple.

I shake my head, then pick up her thong. "That's all, Babydoll. Time to get dressed. You can wear whatever you want, as long as it doesn't include this thong. It's way too grown-up for a babydoll's panties."

Wordlessly, she puts on her dress from last night. I make no secret of checking out her body as she pulls it over her curves. When she struggles with the zipper, I say, "Come here. Daddy will help."

She pads over. I can tell all the daddy stuff is new to her, but she surprisingly doesn't balk. Most women new to the scene seem to feel awkward or unsure. Olivia takes to it naturally.

We would get along so great. Fuck Ryder and his stupid doomsday predictions. Olivia is special, and it isn't just because I gave her a pet name on the dance floor. I inhale her sweet scent mingled with the scents of fucking that linger in the air.

Filthy. Sweet.

My cock twitches. I briefly entertain the fantasy of

pushing her to her knees, feeding my dick into her mouth, watching her lips wrap around me. But we have a chore to do. I zip up her little slip of a dress then trace the top over the curves of her breasts.

"Daddy," she says. Her voice is soft, just like her skin.

"Time to go," I say abruptly. Standing in this room with her is too much of a temptation.

Ryder

I fucking hate the city. It's full of people. Desperate people—and I don't just mean the poor or the people who don't have homes. The rich people are some of the most desperate people I've ever met. They're desperate for more money, more power, more admiration.

I should know, because I'm one of them. Fuck.

This cynicism isn't like me. Nor is the self-hatred. But I haven't been able to sleep since going to that club and finger-fucking the most exquisite woman I've ever laid eyes on. She smelled like cotton candy and licorice, and her pussy gripped my fingers like a tight little vise, fluttering over me in a way that had my dick damn near exploding in my pants.

If only Jax hadn't given her his card. If he hadn't done that, I could have let her fall back into the sea of anonymous women. I could have let go of any twisted fantasy involving her calling him and asking to hook up again. I could have forgotten all about her.

I catch my reflection in the café windows as I walk up to it. I look pissed. No wonder, because I'm lying to myself. Dishonesty pisses me off, especially when I know better.

"Hi, Ryder," the barista says when I step up to the counter.

"Felicity, hey. How's it going?"

"Good, good." She winks and takes my order. "I saw you at Vice last night. Looked like you were having fun."

While I stuff some bills in the tip jar, I give her a look because I can see where this is going. "That's all it was. A good time at the club. And how are you even awake and looking so hot this morning? You were still serving drinks when I left."

"Have to pay for med school somehow," she says.

She tries to push my generous tip back in my hand, but I refuse to take it.

"Med school," I say. "One of these days you'll be saving my ass in the ER."

"Thanks, Ryder." She tucks the bills into the jar.

I wish I could do more for her—she's been serving coffee nearly every morning at this little corner café since I moved to this godforsaken city. But she won't take what she views as charity. The least I can do is chat with her and tip well every day.

My coffee pleasantly burns as it goes down my throat. I live for this moment every morning. The only better wake-up is to a fine ass pressed against my cock. I can remember one ass in particular, how tight it was against me last night as we danced.

I should go back to the cabin. Jerk off again. But Jaxon wants me here for the business, so I drove back, and now I'm cranky as fuck.

The drive to the office is quiet because it's still pretty

early, and a Saturday. I wonder what Jaxon has in store for us today. Some kind of high-profile client, he'd said. He wanted me to work up the schematics for monitoring their property, then he wanted to go over them together, search for weaknesses. We could make any number of our team members do this kind of work, but for special cases, Jaxon prefers a more hands-on approach.

As I park the car, I see an auburn-haired woman stepping into the elevator. I practically trip in my haste to reach her, then realize, too late, that it wasn't the babydoll from the club.

I really need to get laid so I can fuck this nonsense out of my system.

9

Olivia

The last thing in the world that I want to do is face Daniel. Talk about a buzz-kill. But Jaxon drives us back to my apartment building and marches me past the doorman and into the elevator.

I'm totally doing the slut strut, wearing a club dress early on a Saturday morning, and normally I might feel self-conscious. But not today, not with Jaxon at my side, looking tall and forbidding.

I lead him down my hallway and up to my apartment door, then point to it.

"Knock on the door," he says. "Ask to talk."

When this is over, somehow I'll have to tell Jaxon how grateful I am that he's taking charge like this, telling me what to do. I know this is something I need to learn to do on my own, but right now? I need it. I need his instruction and his domineering presence.

Knocking on the door, I say, "Daniel? Let me in—we need to talk."

Nothing happens, no sound of movement or anything inside, not even a "fuck you, bitch," like he'd muttered at me when I left for the club last night.

I never should have left him in my place to pack his things. Too late, I realize how stupid that was.

"Daniel," I say more forcefully, and knock harder. "Let's talk. Open the door."

When he doesn't answer, I try the knob even though I know it will be locked.

It isn't locked.

Surprised, I push open the door.

"Wait," Jaxon says, sidling past me to step inside.

I don't know how long I'm expected to wait, but it's my damn apartment, so I push the door open wider and step inside after Jaxon.

The place is trashed. Clothes, furniture, papers, food, and books have been thrown everywhere. Daniel wasn't looking for something, and it doesn't seem like this was done by burglars or anything like that. No, he was purposefully trying to destroy every single thing that I own.

It is all completely, utterly wrecked.

And it smells like shit and piss.

Gagging, I turn around and go back into the hallway.

Jaxon follows me, already dialing a number on his phone. "Yeah," he says, "I need to report an incident. If we could talk with Detective Baldwin, that would be perfect."

Olivia

Two hours later, we're done talking with Jaxon's police officer friend, Carl Baldwin. Jaxon and I look at each other outside of the station, blinking in the bright midday light. I'm still wearing last night's dress, and no underwear because Jaxon pocketed my thong before we left his place. It feels strangely erotic knowing he's holding my panties in his pocket while my pussy is bare.

The reason I didn't get any clothes from my apartment was that Daniel had taken every single item from my dresser and closet, thrown it into a pile, and pissed all over it.

I rub my hands over my arms, shivering despite the warm weather.

"New clothes," Jaxon says. "But first, I have to make a call."

Pointing to the bottom of the steps in front of us, I say, "I'll wait over there."

"You'll do no such thing, Babydoll," he says, grabbing my upper arm and tugging me close to his body. "I want you next to me."

The tightness in my chest loosens—it's nice to feel protected and wanted, especially after all the horrible things I had to catalogue in my apartment.

Jaxon takes out his phone and makes a call. "Yeah, about that."

There's a pause while the other person speaks.

"I can't make it today, something came up. I know. So go back to your cabin or wherever. The team can handle the schematics.... No, I wouldn't be doing this for a piece of ass, dickhead. It's important.... Yeah, fuck you, too."

Despite the angry words, he's smiling when he ends the call and slides the phone back in his pocket.

At my questioning look, he says, "Colleague. Friend. Asshole. That's Ryder."

I laugh and slide my hand into his outstretched one, and we walk to his car, which is parked down the block.

Halfway there, I stop suddenly.

"What is it?" Jaxon asks.

"My apartment," I say. "I can't go back. Shit." My mind is whirling. I can't move in with my mom. For one thing, she lives an hour away, and I have classes. For another, she doesn't want me around. Samantha would be the obvious choice, but she's already got four roommates in a three-bedroom apartment—two of them share a room, and one sleeps in the living room. There isn't even a couch for me to crash on.

"I'll help you," Jaxon says simply.

"You barely know me." I'm mentally going through my list of friends, but Samantha's pretty much it. I haven't been close to anyone else, partly because soon after starting the art program, I met Daniel, and all of my time was spent with him.

Maybe I could sleep in my art studio. Bring in a sleeping bag. It would be great for actually finishing my final project.

"Doesn't matter how well I know you," Jaxon says. "I'm in a position to help you, and so I will."

"What are you saying?" I ask. "Do you have an extra apartment somewhere?"

"No. You can stay with me."

This is way, *way* too fast. "I don't think so. That's a terrible idea."

"Why?"

"Because we've had sex. We just met last night. We don't even know each other."

"I know your spirit, Olivia," he says, his eyes on mine. "I think this is the best idea I've ever had. And I've had a lot of good ideas. I'm very...creative."

Of course he would have to make this conversation sexy. He's unbelievable. And as much as I wanted him to take charge earlier, I realize I need to set some limits. Right now, right here.

"Fine," I say, hardly believing the word as it leaves my mouth. "Fine. I'll stay with you, in your guest room. But on one condition—we have to stop sleeping together."

He raises his eyebrows, and his chocolate brown eyes are wide in disbelief. "Well, that doesn't make any sense."

"Yes, it does. I'm paying rent, and I'm not taking hand-outs. I have money. Or rather, my mom has a little. But I'm also not mixing...um...sexytimes with our living arrangement."

Subtly shaking his head, he says, "All right, Babydoll. You call the shots. But if you change your mind, well, you'll know where my bed is. And I'll be lying in it, waiting for you."

10

____

Jaxon

The trunk of my car is stuffed full of clothes for Olivia. She was stubborn and wouldn't let me pay for them, claiming she has plenty of money. From the way she blinked in surprise at one of the totals, she doesn't have as "plenty" as she thought.

"Okay, one more stop," I say, steering us down the block.

"I have all I need," she argues, resisting the way I guide her along with my hand on her back.

"Maybe so," I say, "but I want to buy you some things, and—"

"And no." She twists away from my hand.

"And yes."

"What do you think are you, my sugar daddy?" she asks, staring hard at me.

I laugh. "Trust me—my brand of _daddy_ doesn't come with much sugar."

"We're not doing any of that sexy stuff," she says. "Remember?"

I look up and down the crowded city street, frowning. She did mention something like that. Our chemistry is so good, I don't think any sort of distance between us will last, and that's why I keep forgetting. Or maybe it's sheer stubbornness on my part—I want to believe that she'll be warming my cock again tonight and I'll be driving her wild, making her wait for the fucking.

"Yes, I remember," I finally say. "We need to eat, though. Can I take you to dinner—*as friends*? In a friendly way? Or do you want to take it down a notch and simply be roommates? Because roommates eat together sometimes, too."

Pursing her lips, she says, "I suppose we can be friends."

She's so fucking cute when she thinks she's in charge.

Ryder

A hundred bucks says Jaxon's spending the day with the chick from the club last night. If I'm wrong, I'll buy him a bottle of his favorite whiskey.

He's not going to come right out and tell me, though. So in order to figure out whether I'm right or wrong, it means I have to do a little recon.

I start by swinging by his place. I use the code for the penthouse suite and let myself in. I sleep here almost as much as he does, so it's not as if I'm breaching his privacy.

The living room is empty and all is silent, but I take a look around.

The guest room, which is where I usually crash when I stay here, has rumpled sheets and it smells like sex. Not just any sex. Sweet babydoll sex.

Motherfucker. I knew it.

No whiskey for Jaxon. In fact, he should be giving *me* whiskey. I go to his liquor cabinet, pull down the half of a bottle that remains of his favorite brand. Then I find a pen and notepad in one of the kitchen drawers. I write, *I made a bet with myself that if you weren't with "Babydoll," I'd buy you a bottle. Looks like I was right, though, and you are with her. The whiskey's mine, asshole.*

Then I prop the message up in the liquor cabinet where his bottle had been sitting.

I go back into the guest room, take a swig of whiskey, and inhale. Candied sweetness. My dick is as hard as a fucking tire iron. She smells so damn good. I remember how her pussy felt on my fingers, and I'm imagining how it felt to Jaxon when she was on Jaxon's cock. While he's pounding into her, maybe she'll take me in her mouth.

Fuck it. I take another swig of whiskey, then set down the bottle. I unfasten my pants, take out my dick, and fist it while I stare at the rumpled sheets. I'm imagining her on those sheets on her hands and knees, wearing a sweet little nightie, something girlie like what Jaxon would buy for her. My red handprint would be on her ass because I'd have found some reason or another to give her a spanking.

Jerking myself off to the vision, I breathe in her sweet scent. And when I come in my hand, I say one word. "Babydoll."

Olivia

I don't know what Jaxon's game plan is, but he is pulling out all the stops. The restaurant isn't fancy as far as dress code, which is a good thing because my shopping trip for essentials did not include an evening gown. But it's one of the most difficult places to get into in San Esteban.

I'm wearing a deep purple wrap dress that looks professional and sexy all at once. It was my favorite purchase today, and it'll be perfect for my final project presentation, which is coming up in two weeks.

Thank heavens my apartment wasn't big enough for doing anything other than sketching out my sculptures. Those are safe in the university's art building. As a senior, I have my own mini studio.

As Jaxon and I walk into the restaurant, he doesn't put his hand on my lower back like he'd been doing before. He doesn't send me flirty little smiles. He doesn't call me *babydoll*.

And...I kind of don't like this.

"Something wrong?" Jaxon asks as I push food around on my plate.

"Do you mean other than the fact that my ex trashed my apartment and did some unspeakable things to my belongings?"

Anger flashes in his eyes, but it's gone in a second. He nods. "Yes, other than that."

"No, everything's peachy other than that."

He gives me an evaluating look, as if trying to decide what I'm hiding from him, if anything, then nods in satisfaction. "Okay, Olivia, if you say so. Tell me about your work."

"My work? Oh. I'm a student."

"Grad school?"

"Undergrad."

"Shit, how old are you?"

I smirk. "I'm about to turn twenty-two. Is that too young for you, old man?"

"Be careful, Olivia," he says, his voice rougher than it was a moment ago. "You're playing with fire."

"Sorry," I say. My skin feels as if I just got very close to that proverbial fire. I take a giant gulp of ice water, hoping to cool off. It almost works.

We talk about my art, and it's crazy the kinds of questions he asks—like he actually knows about art and cares about it. He tells me a little about his firm, Ironwood Security. It's all I can do not to make a dick joke about "Ironwood."

He calls for the check and waves me off when I reach for my purse. "My treat," he says. "As your friend."

The words come out of his mouth casually, but then they squat between us like ugly little monsters. He's not happy that I put a stop on our bedroom adventures. I'm not exactly thrilled, either, but if he's renting a room to me in his fine-ass penthouse, I don't want to screw things up by getting involved.

His particular brand of kink scares me. Not because it's too dark or too dangerous or too sinfully sexy. But because I can easily see myself getting pulled in. Not just for a fling, but for life.

Our ride back to the penthouse is quiet. I watch the city streets go by, appreciating the way the lines and the colors have shifted and changed with shadows over the course of the day.

When we get back to the penthouse, Jaxon helps me carry the bags to the guest room. All I can think about is what happened between us the last time we were in here. I stare at the messy bed, thinking of how he'd lain on his back, letting me fuck him as fast or as slow as I'd wanted. I think about the bite of pain as he'd pinched my nipples, and the way the pain had quickly transformed to liquid warmth spreading through my body, concentrating at my core.

A smile plays on his lips now, as he stares at me. It's as if he knows exactly what's going through my mind.

"Do you want something to drink?" he asks, walking back out of the room.

Damn him and his sexy ass.

"No, thanks," I say, but I follow him out.

He moves to a cabinet filled with gleaming bottles. Plucking a notepad out of it, he chuckles softly.

"What is it?" I ask.

"My business partner came by while we were out, stole my whiskey."

He doesn't seem that upset about it, so it must not be like the situation I had with Daniel.

"I need to let him know I've rented out his bedroom."

It takes a moment for the words to sink in. "Wait, I didn't know I'd be ousting someone else when I agreed to stay here. I can find another place—"

"I have two extra bedrooms, Olivia," he says. "Ryder can sleep in the other one."

"Or I can sleep in the other one," I offer. "I hate the idea of kicking someone out of their own room."

He shakes his head. "He just crashes here a lot. Most nights, actually. But he has his own place outside of the city."

"Should I move anything of his out of there before I go to sleep?" I ask. Like, perhaps, his condoms, lube, candy, and what looked like rope and some jewelry.

"No, you can leave it." Jaxon's voice is smug.

He thinks I'm going to cave. He thinks the two of us might be needing those items again.

He is oh, so very wrong.

11

———

Olivia

I wake up alone in my bed on Sunday. The difference from yesterday causes a veil of loneliness to creep over me, more stifling than the down comforter pulled up to my waist.

The memory of yesterday morning sparkles in my mind like a forbidden gem. I reach for it and allow snippets to flash through my head. My core hums with need.

The bedroom door is closed, so I reach for the waistband of my underwear and slide my hand inside, my fingers gently playing over my clit. I'm already so wet, just with the thoughts of yesterday morning. Warming Daddy's—no, *Jaxon's*—cock. The way he'd made me wait, how I had thought I would explode with desire. The taste of butterscotch on my tongue, the taste of his kiss against my mouth. The way he'd filled me, so fully and completely. His strong arms wrapped around me, holding me in place. I'd felt safe. Cherished. Owned.

I move my fingers faster over my clit, wishing so hard I had his cock inside of me right now. I focus on that, on how he felt inside of me, and I use my other hand to pinch one of my nipples—hard, just the way he did it.

Then I explode, arching upward before falling back and settling against the bed once more.

Fucking hell. If thoughts of what we did before can get me off that quickly, just imagine what could happen if I had the real thing again.

After my heart rate slows down, I climb out of bed and take a shower, hoping to wash away the lustful thoughts.

The attempt is not at all successful.

When I finally emerge from the bedroom, with wet hair and in new clothes, Jaxon is in the kitchen. He, too, is freshly showered, and he looks scrumptious in a pair of gray slacks and a black button-down shirt.

"Good morning, Olivia," he says.

How can three words from him make me feel wet and needy all over again? I should turn right back around, climb into my bed, and have another round with myself. Instead, I clear my throat and say, "Good morning, Jaxon."

"I made some extra smoothie in case you want some."

"Oh, I usually just have a coffee," I say.

He purses his lips, like that isn't a good response, and for some crazy reason, I want to please him. Not just impress him because he's hot and he's my new roommate and I just had sex with him yesterday, but there's an achy spot inside of me that will only be soothed with his approval.

"If there's extra, though, I'd love to try it."

"Of course." He doesn't smile, but he quickly pours a light green concoction from the blender into a pint glass. Handing the glass to me, he says, "Bon appétit."

"Thanks." I take a sip. It's sweet and tart, not bad at all.

"What's on your agenda for today?" he asks, taking a sip of his own smoothie.

"I'll head to school and work in my studio, put the finishing touches on my sculptures and work on my presentation."

"Good," he says. "I have to head into the office. I'll drop you off."

"Oh, is your office close to the San Esteban School of the Arts?"

"Close enough." He smirks.

Meaning, it isn't close at all, but he's going to drive me around anyway. "You don't have to take care of me, you know."

"I don't know if I told you," he says, "but my work is in the security sector. Personal security. And I didn't like the look of what that asshole did to your apartment. So if you don't mind humoring me, I'd like to be as involved as you'll let me in getting you to and from school."

All traces of flirtation are gone. He's not doing this to get in my pants again; he's doing it because he cares and he's taking Daniel's vandalism seriously.

"Thank you," I say, meaning it and hoping my sincerity shows.

Maybe we'll really succeed at being friends and roommates, and not lovers.

A small voice in my head asks, *But why can't we be all three?*

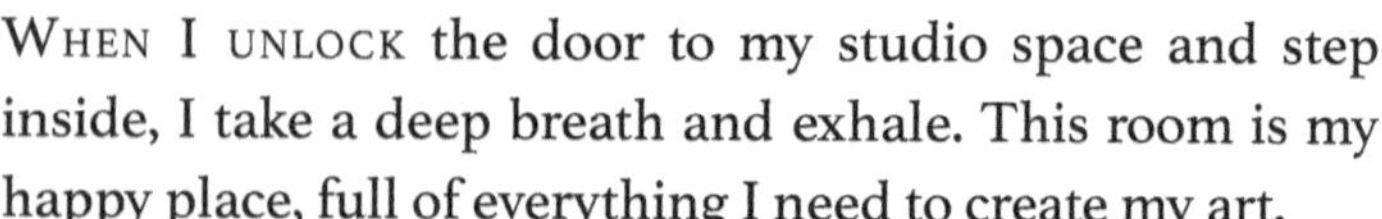

WHEN I UNLOCK the door to my studio space and step inside, I take a deep breath and exhale. This room is my happy place, full of everything I need to create my art.

My mother might not love my pursuit of this degree, thinking it frivolous, but I'm damn good at what I do. The abstract lines and shapes of my sculptures make sense to me in a way that nothing else ever will.

I circle the largest one, which rests on a big crate in the center of the room. The glaze shines beautifully. I knew this piece would turn out well, that I'd applied every different aspect with care and attention. But seeing it here, a finished sculpture that seems to undulate with its own beauty and power, surprises me. Did I really create this? The clay arches and spirals around, and the celadon on the underside contrasts beautifully with the copper coloring above.

Creating this piece was hard, but fun.

Sitting down to write about it is just going to be hard.

Still, my presentation is two weeks away, so it's best to get it done. I pull my laptop from my messenger bag— grateful, once again, that I stored it here instead of in my apartment. Finding a floor cushion in the corner, I drag it in front of the window so the natural light will illuminate the sculpture. While the laptop whirs to life, I stare thoughtfully at the sculpture in the middle of the room.

It doesn't even have a name. Not yet. I'm not sure what to call it.

The spiraling arches are made of two abstract forms. The resulting intertwined piece is sensual—more sensual than I'd originally intended. Still, I can't deny that the sensuality of the piece is a huge part of its power. It draws the eye.

Looking down at my laptop, I try to put those feelings into words. Somehow, I need to convey to my senior committee the reasoning behind my creation, and where I think it succeeds, where it fails.

I'm midway through a sentence about how I struggled with getting the glaze right when a prickly feeling skitters down my back. I shrug, trying to dispel it so I can remember the rest of the sentence that I was trying to write.

The feeling doesn't go away; instead, it intensifies. I pull one of the hair sticks from my bun and use it to scratch my back, but that doesn't help. Irritated, I lose my focus entirely on the laptop and frown. It's only then that I focus on what the skittery, itchy feeling is telling me.

I'm being watched.

I whirl around, hoping to catch the person in the act. But the school quad out the window behind me is full of students studying, either lying in the grass or beneath the shade of several large oaks that dot the campus. Nobody seems specifically focused on me.

Laughing to myself for my paranoia, I return to the laptop.

But I can't shake the feeling.

If there were curtains or blinds over the windows, I'd sacrifice the natural sunlight and pull them just to dispel this weird feeling. But there isn't anything I can use.

Totally creeped out, I grab my phone. I'd been able to charge it at Jaxon's, thankfully.

The only person I want to talk to right now is Jaxon. I want to hear his deep voice and let it ground me to reality.

Although my heart's pounding faster than usual, I dial his number.

"Hey," he says warmly.

"Hi, it's Olivia."

"I know, Babydoll. You okay?"

Ignoring the fact that he called me *babydoll* again, I say, "Yeah. Just wanted to..."

Then I stop. Because that's a lie. I am over-the-top freaked out.

"I'm freaked out," I say.

"What's going on?"

"I know it's stupid, but I feel like someone's watching me."

There's no pause. He just says, "I'll be right there."

"Wait, you don't have to—"

"What building, which room?"

"Cassiopeia. Room twelve. But really, Jaxon, it isn't necessary—"

But the line is dead. He's on his way.

I keep my phone in my hand. His urgency has me even more freaked out for some reason. If he's taking this so seriously, maybe I should, too.

A knock on the door makes me jump. He couldn't be here already.

"Olivia? You there?" It's Samantha's voice.

"Yeah, come in," I say. Thank goodness—company.

"I know you're trying to work," she says, sashaying through the door, "but I have *got* to tell you about Bartender Boy."

Taking in my face, she stops.

"You okay?"

I nod. "I think so. I was just getting freaked out. But I'm fine now."

"Okay, because listen. Ben the Bartender Boy is hot AF, and he's already called me back and asked to see me again!"

"That's awesome," I say, and I mean it. She's had a long string of duds. If Ben the bartender is even half as great as she thinks he is right now, that'll make him a hundred times better than her last boyfriend.

She regales me with the tale of her exploits with Ben, sharing more details than I really need, but that's her way. We analyze Ben's likelihood of being "the one," because despite Samantha's relentless search of her next orgasm, she really does want to find the one guy to rule them all.

And then the door bangs open and Jaxon's standing there, fists clenched, looking around the room like he's ready to tear someone apart.

12

———

Olivia

Samantha squeaks, hand flying to her mouth, then she looks at me with wide eyes.

I clear my throat. "Samantha, meet Jaxon. Jaxon, Samantha."

"I remember you from the club," Samantha says, walking over to shake his hand. Then she turns to me and gives me the stink-eye, the one that says *you better explain yourself young lady and you better do it soon.*

I wince, but Jaxon laughs.

"I don't know if Olivia told you," he says, "but she had a minor problem getting into her apartment."

"We hadn't gotten to that yet," I say, looking at Samantha. "Daniel locked me out while he completely trashed the place. My phone battery was dead and Jaxon here had given me his card. His was the only phone number I had."

"I see," she says, flicking her gaze between Jaxon and me.

Jaxon's face is impassive as he moves to the window and looks outside—not at the people relaxing on the quad, but at the ground immediately on the other side of the building. He frowns.

"Olivia, if you're ready to go, I can take you home. If you want to stay out longer, I only ask that you let me call a few of my men to be on security detail."

"Security detail? What?" Samantha squawks.

Jaxon clenches his jaw—I can see the ripple of movement behind the beard on his cheeks. "I believe her ex's behavior is more than just a violation of her property. He —or someone else—is violating her privacy, as well."

"What are you talking about?" I ask.

Now that he's here, I'm brave enough to go to the window again and look out. Samantha comes with me.

Jaxon points down at the ground, where footprints are indented firmly into the soft earth. Samantha gasps, but I'm too shocked to react.

Then he raises his finger and points to something else —a tiny camera affixed to the corner of the windowsill.

~

Ryder

When the text comes from Jaxon, I'm not surprised. I stole his whiskey, after all, and no doubt after a long day, he'd gone straight for the bottle for his customary glass before bed. So I'm ready for anger.

I'm not ready for that anger to be directed at an

outside threat. I'm not ready to read the subtext of fear in his words.

Some asshole is stalking Babydoll.

And I'm definitely not ready for the pulse of rage that washes through me when I comprehend the message. Some asshole is stalking our girl? I'll fucking rip him apart. Fucker better be ready for pain, because I will dish it out.

Then I realize, I'm just as possessive of her as Jaxon is.

In my mind just now, I called her *our girl.*

Fuck. I slam my hand down on my desk and spin to face the office windows. The city is lit up for Saturday night—swanky clubs with subtle lighting, bass pounding out rhythms through the sidewalks, a carnival of carnal desires.

I turn back to the desk and pick up my phone so I can respond to Jaxon. Chest heaving, I type out, *I'll work up a security plan. Where does she live?*

His response is immediate. *At the moment, she lives with us.*

He's got to be kidding.

Fuck it. I text back, *I'm coming over.*

～

Olivia

Jaxon grimaces at his phone and looks up. I quickly return to looking at the book open in front of me. It's an art history book I found on his shelves, and I haven't read it before. It isn't a super comprehensive treatment of the topic, but I'm mostly staring at the images, anyway.

"What's up, Olivia?" Jaxon asks.

"Just looking at your book. I didn't know you were into art."

"It was my mother's," he says. "She taught art history at the university."

"Taught?" I ask.

"She passed two years ago. Cancer."

"Fuck cancer," I say automatically.

"Did you lose someone, too?" he asks.

"My dad. I don't remember him—I was only three."

He nods. "Fuck cancer."

I allow my gaze to linger on his face—his strong jaw, decorated in the neatly-trimmed beard that I long to rub my hand over. His dark eyes, boring into mine. The slight smile on his lips, the one that says he knows I want him.

The smile falls, and he says, "I should give you a head's up. My buddy Ryder is coming by. He's a bit of a grouch."

"I can deal with grouches, no problem," I say. "Or I can make myself scarce."

"It would be better if you were here in the living room with us. We're going to be discussing security for you."

"Look, I appreciate it, but I really don't need security."

He shakes his head. "I would feel better if you had it. It's a gut feeling, and my gut's rarely wrong. So humor me."

"Fine." I shrug. If some suited goons want to tail me to school and back, I'm not going to stop them.

"There's something else you should know—"

But then the elevator dings across the room, and someone steps out of it. Someone just as large as Jaxon, whose stare fixes me in place with the same kind of command and authority.

Jaxon continues, "Ryder is the guy you danced with at the club."

Fuck. Me.

Wait, he already did. With his fingers. While Jaxon was right in front of us, holding my throat, kissing me.

I didn't get a good look at Ryder's face that night. The lights were dim, and he was behind me. But he's just as breathtakingly handsome as Jaxon. His eyes are lighter, his hair slightly longer and a lighter brown. His body is just as big, just as muscular. My pussy tingles as I remember the feeling of being sandwiched between these two strong men.

I can't stop staring at him.

"Olivia," Jaxon is saying, and from the exasperated tone, I get the sense that he's said it a few times, trying to get my attention. Finally, he says sharply, "Babydoll."

I look away from Ryder and over to Jaxon, startled. Jaxon is smirking. I feel my face flush and I lift up a hand, hoping to cool my cheeks and hide their redness.

"Cute," Ryder says, but he's talking to Jaxon, not to me. "I can see why you brought her home."

A heavy pain works its way up my throat at his words. He's talking about me as if I'm not here, as if he didn't have his hands all over me last night, as if none of that meant anything at all to him.

It probably didn't.

And that hurts worst of all.

Ryder walks to the coffee table in front of me and sets down a folder of papers that I hadn't noticed he was holding. Jaxon picks them up and leafs through them.

"I want Terrence taking the lead," he says.

"Terrence is on the Velasquez detail," Ryder says.

"Then pull him off," Jaxon says. "I want him with Olivia."

Ryder folds his arm across his chest. "I hardly think we send out our best guy to protect her from an amateur stalker. The senator—"

"The senator will be fine with someone else on lead. Our men can run his detail in their sleep."

"Fine." Ryder puts his hands up in the air. "Terrence it is."

When he spins around and stalks back to the elevator, Jaxon says, "Where the hell do you think you're going?"

"Home."

"Stay here, asshole. It's late. I can use your help tomorrow."

I wish I was anywhere but in the middle of this. Jaxon said they were friends, but they seem to hate each other. But then Ryder turns back to us and his gaze lands on me, and I realize the truth. It isn't Jaxon he hates—it's me.

I gasp and fold my arms in front of me, trying to brace myself against the animosity swirling throughout the room.

Ryder sighs and looks away from me. He runs a hand through his hair. "Fine."

He's halfway to the hall when Jaxon says, "Olivia's sleeping in your usual room."

A door slams farther down the hall and I'm finally able to exhale. I can't believe I just witnessed that. I can't believe the guy who just had his fingers in my pussy less than forty-eight hours ago looked at me with such loathing, it was like I'm a household pest. A cockroach.

My lungs feel squeezed empty of air. It's hard to breathe, and I pull my arms around myself more tightly.

"Olivia." Jaxon's voice is soft.

"I think—I think I'm ready for bed. Goodnight." I carefully set the art book down on the coffee table, keeping my gaze on the bright cover, which is starting to blur from the tears in my eyes.

"Olivia," he says again.

Standing up, I make my way toward the hall. Jaxon is suddenly in front of me, a wall of man. He reaches out and takes me into his arms.

"He's an asshole, I know," Jaxon says.

"He hates me," I whisper. "What did I do?"

Jaxon nudges my head up with a finger to my chin. "Absolutely nothing, except captivate him."

No, captivation is not at all what I witnessed just now. Disgust, disdain. Loathing.

"Don't cry, Babydoll," he says, then kisses my forehead. "My room is just across the hall."

He points to an open door, and I nod. "Thanks."

"You come get me if you need anything, okay?"

"Okay."

I can feel his gaze, heavy and hot as a brand on my back, as I go into my room and softly close the door behind me.

~

DADDIES' BABYDOLL

1

Ryder

I pace back and forth at the foot of my bed, feeling like a caged animal. Jaxon shouldn't have asked me to stay. That asshole knows exactly what he's doing, trying to tempt me with her. And I know any minute I'm going to hear the sounds of them fucking in the next room. I'm surprised he doesn't have a camera set up and looping to the television screen in this room so I can watch. With our security business, getting our hands on that kind of tech is as easy as streaming a movie.

Genevieve nearly destroyed our friendship. Everything since her has been casual, no-strings. A weekend, tops. No pet names, no promises, no possession.

But now he's flaunting Olivia in my face. And no denying, the sweet little vixen is tempting with her luscious lips, soft skin, and her big gray eyes. I want to take her hair in my fist, swivel her head around so I can kiss and lick her neck while I fuck her ass. I want to do it fast and angry so it hurts in just the way I know she'll like.

I stop pacing and unfasten my jeans. For the second time today, I jack myself off while I think about her.

~

Olivia

The next day is surreal. I thought I wouldn't care about having a security detail trailing after me. They're inconspicuous—not wearing black suits and obvious earpieces or anything like that. To everyone on campus, they probably look like well-muscled, nontraditionally aged college students loitering outside my classrooms.

Even though I don't think anybody else realizes who they are, I know they're there. I ignore them as much as possible. When I reach my art studio in the afternoon, one of them, the black-haired giant who introduced himself as Terrence this morning, stops me before I go inside.

"Ms. Santiago, if you don't mind," he says, stepping in front of me and walking through the room. Satisfied, he turns around and points to the newly-installed blinds. "Open or shut?"

"Shut, please." I'd love the natural sunlight streaming in, but I'm still too scared after yesterday. I hate feeling like this. Weak. Powerless.

Terrence nods and his eyes soften a fraction in understanding. "Ms. Santiago, we're here to protect you and ensure your comfort. There's no shame in being uneasy or scared. We'll be right outside this door. Give us a shout if you need anything."

"Thank you." It helps that he said that. I didn't think it would have, but it does.

The second guy, who simply introduced himself as Squid, gives me a friendly nod, too.

I enter the studio, feeling much better than I had yesterday. I hadn't wanted a security detail, but there's no denying I'm feeling safer and more in control now that I have it.

Olivia

The next few days pass in a similar fashion. Every morning, Jaxon makes me a smoothie. I've grown to like them —my stomach has always been sensitive, but they seem to be helping with that and I have fewer stomachaches. Terrence and Squid are the guys I usually see on my security team, but there's also Cal, Roman, and Hunter. Ryder stays over most nights, but he barely speaks to me, which is fine with me because I have enough stress in my life with trying to finish my final presentation.

I get home before Jaxon or Ryder, so Roman and Terrence, who are on my security detail today, go up with me and check the place out. Once it's clear, they take up their stations outside somewhere, guarding the entrances.

My phone buzzes in my bag, so I fish it out, expecting it to be Samantha demanding an update. She's convinced the whole "no sex" phase with Jaxon will be short-lived, but so far I've held out admirably despite increasing temptation.

Because seriously, I know what the guy can do. And I know that I like it.

When I finally reach my phone, I see that it's my mother calling, instead.

"Mom," I say. "Hey, what's up?"

"I just got back from yoga with Amélie, and I'm concerned." It's so like her to just fly straight on past the greeting and the requisite "how are you" and right to her point. Usually I like that about her. Right now, I'm feeling a little raw.

"Did you hear me?" she says. "I had yoga with Amélie."

Amélie Joboqui, her new bosom friend who also happens to be the Director of Student Affairs at my university. No, they were not friends or even acquaintances before I began taking courses. Mom, in her immense need to act the puppeteer of my life, sought out Amélie soon after I began my freshman year.

"I heard you," I say.

"She mentioned something about your *security detail*, and she was anxious as to what kind of trouble *I* might be in, especially when she noticed I had no security following me."

I sigh. I'm not sure how to explain it. "There's some weirdness with Daniel. We broke up. I'm friends with someone else, who has a security firm, and he's insisting on this detail, just in case."

"Just in case," she says, skepticism weighing on her tone.

"Yep."

There isn't much else to say, but I steer the conversation into other things, like some new legislation she's working on. Before the end of our call, she even remembers to ask me about my final project. So, bonus points for her.

And then she has to ruin it. "If you need to take time off from school because of this thing with Daniel, you know that's all right, don't you?"

"I am nearly finished," I say. "It would be stupid to stop when I'm so close to the end."

"Psh, it's an art degree. It's not like you're pre-med or anything, Olivia."

Translation: what I'm doing isn't important to her or to the world at large.

By the time I finally get off the phone, the sun has gone down and the room is dim. I spout angry curses at the dark furniture, imagining my mother's reaction to the venom pouring from my lips. She has supported me in so many ways and been my champion in so many others. Except when it comes to my art degree.

The elevator door opens and Jaxon steps out. I'm so relieved it isn't Ryder, I rush toward him and give him a hug.

"Hey, what's that for?" he asks.

"I just needed a friend," I say.

His arms are strong around me, his scent a balm. The spark of desire that flares through me isn't unexpected. He ignites me, and he has from the very beginning.

"Talk to me, Olivia," he says in a rough, low voice.

"I don't wanna talk," I say, rubbing my body against his.

He inhales with a hiss of air and I feel his dick harden

against my lower belly. "Babydoll. Are you suggesting what I think you're suggesting?"

I try to think of the best single thing I can say to him, the words he won't be able to refuse. They come to me easily. "Take me, Daddy. Make me feel better."

Jaxon

She's exquisite. I lift her easily, cupping her ass in my hands. She wraps her long legs around my waist. The movement has her panty-clad pussy lined up with my cock, and it's lucky for both of us we have our clothes on, otherwise I'd be sliding into her unsheathed—fucking without a condom for the first time since I was last with my ex-fiancée three years ago.

I fit my mouth over hers, claiming her lips, pressing my tongue inside and tangling it with hers. She tastes like peppermint. Spicy. Hot.

She wants more. I want more. I carry her to the sofa. Slowly, I ease her back down until she's standing in front of me.

There's a condom in my wallet, and I pull it out before handing it to her. Sitting down on the sofa, I say, "Warm Daddy's cock, Babydoll."

"Yes, Daddy." Her eyes are bright and she wears a small smile on her face.

Fuck, she is so eager to please me. She drives me mad with need. It's going to take more than my usual willpower to keep from coming in her tight little pussy as soon as she slides over my dick.

She unfastens my pants, revealing my cock which is hard and ready for her. She licks her lips, just the subtlest touch of her tongue, and I hold back a groan. Then she rolls the condom onto me and leans back.

"Should I take off all my clothes?"

"Just your panties. Leave on the skirt and top."

Reaching beneath her skirt, she pulls down a pair of hot pink satin panties.

"Hand them over," I say, and close my fist around the soft fabric.

She starts to clamber into my lap facing me, but I stop her and spin her around. I want an easier reach to her clit, and this position will provide that.

She's just lowered herself onto my cock, her ass nestled against my abs, when the elevator door slides open in front of us and Ryder steps into the room.

2

———

Jaxon

Predictably, Olivia tries to get up, but I'm faster and I lock her hips down, holding her flush against my lap.

Ryder takes in the scene before him, snorts, and walks into the kitchen. He calls over his shoulder, "Did I interrupt?"

"Not at all," I say, although Olivia makes a soft squeak. She's being very still, a very good girl. If her pussy wasn't squeezing me repeatedly, I'd let her make a quick exit to the guest room to gather herself and we'd resume this later.

But I think she might like this. A lot.

"You all right, Babydoll?" I ask.

"Mm-hmm," she says.

"Is this too much?"

She looks over her shoulder at me. Her pupils are

dilated, her lips slightly parted and still swollen from my kisses. She shakes her head. "No, it isn't too much."

She's even more turned on than she'd been before. I don't want to lose this opportunity.

My little babydoll might like being watched. I make a mental note of that.

Ryder comes out of the kitchen, a beer in hand. "I'll go watch TV in my room."

"If you don't mind, there are some things I wanted to discuss with you."

Olivia makes a soft whimper.

Ryder catches my eye and gives me a subtle nod of understanding. He might not agree with me pursuing something with Olivia, but he knows as much as I do how to read a scene, and he can tell I want to prolong the way she's situated on my lap. It's such a fucking turn-on to feel her enfolding my cock like this, to know she's subtly embarrassed but at the same time aroused.

"Sure," he says, falling into the sofa across from us. His gaze is razor sharp on Olivia for a moment, then he takes a sip of beer and flicks his focus to me. "What's up?"

"Just some work stuff. Has Terrence given you a report?"

Olivia turns around and gives me an affronted look, like she can't believe I'm having this conversation while she sits on my dick. I smile at her and she whips her head back around so fast, her hair lifts with the force.

"I saw him on my way up," Ryder says. "I told him you and I would be here tonight and he could take off."

"Good."

Olivia's back is rising up and down with her rapid breathing. I can tell she's trying to hide her excitement, which is adorable. I smooth a hand over her back, then up her thigh but over the skirt which covers her legs. I don't want to push too far, too fast, but damn if it wouldn't get us both off so hard if I began fucking her right here. Her pussy squeezes me rhythmically—she's close. I bet I can get her off without doing more than flexing my dick. I snake my hand up the back of her shirt and around to the front.

"Jaxon," she breathes.

"I believe the name you're looking for is *Daddy*," I correct.

"Oh my gosh," she says, covering her face with her hands. "Don't say that out loud right now."

Ryder laughs and adjusts his dick through his pants. "Take your hands away from your face, Olivia. I wanted to ask you about your day."

She shakes her head, so I reach up to her bra-clad breasts and pinch one of her nipples underneath her shirt.

"Do as Mr. Ryder says, Babydoll." I don't let go of her nipple until she lowers her hands.

Ryder sends me an irritated look, but I just shrug. If he didn't want to play along, he could've gone straight to his bedroom.

Olivia tries to get off of my lap, but I grab her hips again. "You have a safeword," I growl.

She doesn't utter it.

Fuck yes. I pump into her once before settling back against the couch. Looking over at Ryder, I say, "You had a question for our babydoll?"

Ryder

Olivia's eyes are wild, her pupils dilated so much, she could be high. But I know she isn't. At least not high on any substance. She's high from sex, from lust. The skirt she's wearing hides her pussy from me, but I know what it feels like from touching it last week, and I can just imagine the way it's hugging my friend's dick.

He's in heaven right now.

"Yeah, I do have a question for Olivia," I say in response to Jax's question. "Olivia, how was your day?"

She shakes her head, opens her mouth to say something. All that comes out is a whimper.

"You okay, Olivia?" I ask. "You sound thirsty. Want something to drink?"

"No," she says.

"No, *thank you, Mr. Ryder,*" Jaxon corrects her in a stern voice.

"Oh my gosh," she says, closing her eyes and sounding mortified.

Jaxon and I both chuckle. She's precious.

"Say it," he says.

"No, thank you, Mr. Ryder," she whispers.

A flush covers her neck, dipping beneath her V-neck t-shirt. Jaxon's hand moves under the fabric, cupping one of her breasts. His other hand is locked on her hip, keeping her in place. I'm damn near about to explode in my fucking jeans, watching this.

Her sweet candy scent, the smell that's been taunting me every time I step into this apartment, is stronger than ever. I thought she looked high a minute ago, with her dilated pupils and the crazed, needy expression on her face, but *I'm* the one who feels high. With every breath, I'm closer to finding completion.

"Are her eyes open?" Jaxon asks me.

"No, they're closed."

She opens her eyes and twists her neck around so she can see Jaxon. "That's right. You like eye contact..."

"Right, Babydoll. But you look uncomfortable, turned around like this. How about you make eye contact with Mr. Ryder instead?"

Shaking her head, she makes a strangled whimper.

"Eyes on Mr. Ryder," he says, his voice a command.

She takes a deep breath, turns around, and locks her gaze with mine. Jaxon brings his other hand up inside her shirt—I can see the outlines of his fingers as he massages her perfect tits.

Her gray eyes are gorgeous, full of lust. Her lips are parted. Spots of color dot the apples of her cheeks. Her neck and chest are flushed, too. Soft whimpers fill the room as Jaxon pinches her nipples. I want to be over there, letting her moan around my cock filling her mouth.

She looks like she's about to come, and her focus is wild, disbelieving.

Yes, Babydoll. This is happening, I want to tell her. *Come for your daddies.*

Jaxon moves slightly, probably just a couple of slow pumps of his dick.

And with her eyes on me, Olivia comes apart, gasping, trying to hold it in.

I take another sip of beer, my gaze on hers, trying to pretend that this doesn't affect me.

Jaxon removes his hands from her shirt and rubs

circles on her back. Her eyes are still on me, wide, shocked, like she can't believe she just came on Jaxon's cock while I watched.

If I were less of an asshole, I'd tell her how beautiful she was during her orgasm. I'd kiss her and whisper that I couldn't wait to be inside her.

Instead, I say, "You guys gonna start really fucking now?"

"Probably," Jaxon says. "Wanna watch?"

"Nah." I stand up, holding my half-full beer. "I'll be in my room. I've seen enough."

Olivia

Jaxon doesn't give me the chance to feel awkward about what just happened with Ryder. He lifts me from his lap, spins me around so I'm on all fours, and in one movement, his cock fills me again.

It's dirty, fast. I'm going to come again, I just know it.

He spanks my ass, and the sting hurts in a good way. Then he massages my ass cheek and I feel his thumb wandering dangerously close to my crack.

"No," I whimper.

"*No* isn't your safe word, Babydoll. You really want me to stop?"

I bite my lip.

He stops thrusting within me and his hand goes still on my ass. "Babydoll. Talk to me."

"I'm...I'm not saying my safe word," I say.

Slowly, he pushes fully inside of me with his cock.

And just as slowly, he rubs his thumb around my pussy where we join.

"Nice and wet," he says, then runs it over my crack.

This is so, so dirty. His cock has gone still again. Hot, powerful, filling my pussy as he works his thumb into my ass. I want to bury my face in my hands, pretend this isn't happening, because it's filthy. But I am enjoying it so fucking much.

"You're going to come again, Babydoll. Several times tonight. I'm taking what's due me after you denied us for so long. All fucking week I've been thinking of burying my dick in your sweet little pussy. I've thought about using your mouth, those pouty lips wrapped around my cock. I've thought about having my way with your ass just like this. First with my fingers, and then later, with my cock."

His words wrap around me, and I'm under his spell. Jaxon is my beginning, middle, and end. As he presses his thumb farther in, breaching the tight ring, I stop fighting. I relax into it. It still feels dirty and shameful, and yet I embrace that.

He's my daddy. I don't have to worry about anything else.

"Oh, fuck, Babydoll. I can feel you giving in to me." He starts stroking within me faster. "Fuck. Your submission is everything."

I cry out, carried by sensation.

"Shh, Olivia," he says. "You'll make Mr. Ryder think something is wrong."

But I can't help the wordless cries that come from my mouth.

Jaxon stops stroking momentarily. From the corner of

my eye, I see him grab my panties from the couch where he'd set them. He brings them up to my face. "Open."

I don't question him; I open my mouth.

He stuffs the panties inside. I can still breathe through my mouth and still make noise if I really want to, but they serve as a reminder. If I can't be quiet, he'll make me.

"Is that better, Babydoll?" he asks.

I nod and make an *mm-hmm* sound.

"Good girl." He resumes fucking me. His thumb is solid in my ass, a presence I cannot ignore. I want to come again while being simultaneously terrified of how it's going to feel. When I come apart, will he stay with me to put me back together again?

"I've got you, Olivia," he says, his cock rhythmically moving in and out.

And then he starts moving his thumb.

The underwear in my mouth reminds me not to shout too loudly, but I can't keep silent when the orgasm tears through me, all heat and electricity. Jaxon thrusts harder and harder as my aftershocks rock through me, telling me what a good girl I am and how pleased he is with me. It sparks a third orgasm and I cry out again, forgetting about the need to keep silent.

He takes his thumb from my ass and lifts me up to my knees. One arm is a band around my waist, the other at my throat. Thrusting a few more times, he groans in my ear as he reaches his peak.

"Ah, Olivia. Ah, Babydoll."

3

───────

Olivia

I wake up the next morning in my own bed, not in Jaxon's. I vaguely remember returning to my room in the early hours of morning, my body gloriously sore and well-used. Maybe I should have stayed in his bed, because being apart from him creates a kind of ache in my chest.

I don't know why I felt the need to return to my own room, but I'd woken needing the bathroom, slipped out of Jaxon's bed, and come back here. Will he be mad? I doubt it. I'm not even sure what the etiquette is after calling a man *daddy* and letting him own my body like that for several hours.

And...fuck. I pull a pillow over my face. Ryder saw me come. He sat there and drank his beer like...like I was some kind of show he could watch on TV.

I called him Mr. Ryder. To his face.

Rolling over, I tug the blankets over my head and

blink into the dark cavern I've created. I don't know what kind of freaky life I've started, but it is obvious I am not cut out for this. I'm in so far over my head. Why did Jaxon think I could handle this kind of kink? I don't know what I'm doing and maybe even worse, I'm already falling for him. When he told me I was a good girl last night, it felt so right and real.

But I just can't face Ryder today. Facing Jaxon is questionable enough.

"Olivia." It's Jaxon's voice, and it sounds like he's standing in the doorway.

I don't move. If I'm completely still, maybe he'll think I'm asleep.

"Don't try my patience, Babydoll."

There's no way that he can know I'm awake, so I double down and force my breathing to remain deep and even.

He gives a deep sigh and the bed sinks on one side where he sits down. Then the covers are ripped from over my head.

I turn, stretch, and blink at him.

A scowl mars his beautiful face. His beard twitches as he smiles, though. "You know I'm not fooled for a second, I hope."

"Huh?" I stretch again, hoping that the bottom of my sleep camisole rides up enough to distract him.

"Punishing you is going to be so damn fun this morning."

I try to sound puzzled. "I don't know what you're talking about."

He gives a little laugh. "Up, now. Over my lap."

"No, thank you."

"I wasn't asking, sweetheart." There's a new edge in his voice.

I gulp. "But—"

"Yep, your *butt*. Up on my lap. Right fucking now. I'm disappointed, Olivia. I woke up to you gone, which was not what I'd hoped for, but I'm a big guy and I can take it. But when I came in here to talk to you about it, you pretended to be sleeping. That's not cool, Babydoll."

He's right. I should've faced him. Talked, like a responsible person. This whole interaction underlines what I'd been thinking—I am not cut out for a relationship like this.

He raises his eyebrows, waiting for me to comply.

Tears filling my eyes, I scramble to where he sits and dutifully try to arrange myself over his legs.

Smoothing his hands over my ass, which is still clad in sleep shorts and a pair of panties, he says, "I missed waking up with you this morning."

"I did, too," I say.

He peels my shorts and underwear down, then resumes rubbing my ass cheeks.

"Why didn't you stay with me?"

"I got up to pee," I say, "then, I don't know. I thought maybe I should stay in my own room."

"Fair enough."

Crack. I hear the sound before pain blossoms from the stinging slap.

"Ouch," I say, but the pain is tolerable. What's surprising is the fact that I start getting wet. I'm grateful my legs are pressed together so he can't see my pussy lips, which are probably glistening with arousal.

"You are welcome to stay with me in my bed in the

future," Jaxon says. "We should've talked about it before going to sleep, but of course I assumed you would know. But talking is important."

"Yes, I agree," I say.

Another spank lands hard on my backside, and I jerk forward. He steadies me with one hand firm on my lower back, then smooths his other hand over the sting.

"Do you agree, truly?" he asks. "Because you didn't seem to want to talk to me when I came in here."

He spanks me again, three times in rapid succession.

I cry out, surprised at the pain.

But wetter than before.

From the corner of my eye, I catch movement. Ryder walks past, glances into the room at me draped over Jaxon's lap, my panties and sleep shorts around my knees, and keeps walking.

Why does his disinterest hurt so much? It's humiliating, that's for sure. But there's more to it than that.

Jaxon spanks me again. "Ah, Babydoll, don't worry about him."

Then he smooths his hand over my ass, down the crease between my cheeks and to my pussy. His fingers are hot and magical the way they play me to a new orgasm.

I forget to worry about Ryder, because everything is Jaxon. And he is everything.

～

Ryder

Olivia spends every night in Jaxon's room now. He smirks at me each time he sees me, the fucker.

On Thursday afternoon, he steps into my office. I glance up from the map of a film star's estate that I'm checking for weaknesses. From the looks of it, at least three more cameras are needed to eliminate blind spots in security monitoring.

Jaxon clears his throat.

"What is it?" I ask, trying to sound bored.

"How long are you going to resist her?" he asks.

I look up. "What are you talking about?"

"You know."

Shaking my head, I turn back to the computer screen. "Just because you're acting like a kid with a shiny new toy doesn't mean *I* need to."

"She is perfect for us, Ryder."

"Maybe for you. Maybe I'm done with the whole sharing thing." It's a lie, and he knows it. But I'm not giving up. If he knew what kind of secret I was keeping, if he knew what nearly happened three years ago....

He growls and paces in front of my desk. "Stop being a dickhead and give up already."

"She's got you wrapped around her little finger. Why the fuck would I want to be like you?"

"You mean *happy*?" he asks.

"Fuck you. If you're happy, it's fleeting."

"It's not." Jaxon gives me a long, serious look. "And when you finally come around, you're going to be pissed that you waited so long."

I seriously doubt that, but I give him a sarcastic wave as he leaves.

Ryder

When my phone buzzes that evening, I'm still at the office. The caller ID reads *Terrence Johnson*.

"Callihan here," I say.

"Ryder, wanted to give you a head's up. We lost sight of Olivia ten minutes ago at a campus party—"

My heart leaps into my fucking throat and tries to lodge there. I swallow it down and grit out, "Tell me the address."

He rattles it off and I'm already at the elevator at the end of the hall.

"Tell me everything," I say.

"Student party, she wanted to go, Jaxon gave the go-ahead on the condition that she never leaves our sight."

"Where's Jaxon?"

"Not answering his phone."

Fuck. "I'm ten minutes away."

4

Ryder

When I get to the part of campus where Olivia is, I illegally park and jump out of my car. Terrence is at the front of a house teeming with coeds, pointing two more of our guys inside. He's doing the right thing guarding the front, and I'm certain someone else is guarding the back. Our men are well-trained. What the fuck was Jaxon thinking? Olivia should've had more guards if she was going to something like this.

Terrence waves me past and I take the porch steps in a single jump. It's not until I'm inside that I realize Terrence was trying to pass me an earpiece so we could communicate. It wouldn't have mattered, though; the music in here is too loud.

I never understood parties like this. Yeah, the point is to get drunk, have fun, and get laid. But it's impossible to talk or communicate at all when music blares at this level.

Skipping the first floor, which I know all of our guys would have swept at least once, I look toward the stairs. I'd be surprised if we don't already have three guys busting in on every room up there. There's got to be someplace else.

"Hey," I yell, grabbing a guy with shaggy blond hair, "is there a basement?"

He shrugs and mouths something at me, so I grab another guy, this one with dreads, and repeat my question.

"Yeah," he says.

"Where?"

He points down a hallway that's lit with a black light. I take off running, pushing past a line of people waiting for the bathroom.

There's a door at the end and I yank on the handle. Locked.

"Hey, that's not a bathroom, asshole!" someone shouts, and a few people laugh.

Ignoring them, I kick open the door.

"Badass," someone calls behind me.

The door opens to a darkened stairwell, but faint light illuminates the bottom steps. If I had an earpiece, maybe I could call for back-up, but I'm not wasting the time with that now. I have a feeling this is where Olivia is.

When I thunder down the steps, a guy looks up from where he's sitting next to her on a ratty old couch. Olivia's eyes are open, but glassy. Her dress is rumpled, hiked halfway up her legs. She's not aware of what's going on, not really. The guy has spiky blond hair and an ugly-as-fuck goatee. He's holding her hand and I know she'd never be okay with that if she was truly awake. Not with this guy, not with a total stranger—definitely not when she's with Jaxon.

"What the fuck are you doing with her?" I ask.

He stands up and shakes out his arms and shoulders. "Who are you?"

"Who are you, and what are you doing with Olivia?"

"I was just trying to help her feel better," the guy says, right before I punch him in the face.

He goes down, holding his nose and whimpering.

My knuckles ache from the impact. Doesn't matter. The guy's too much of a fucking coward to come back at me. I probably shouldn't have hit him, but he deserved it.

I'll have our men deal with him in a minute. First, I need to help Olivia.

After I straighten her dress, I get my arms underneath her and lift her from the couch.

"Ryder," she says, patting my chest. "You still mad at me?"

"I was never mad at you, Babydoll," I say.

She sighs and nuzzles against my neck.

I carry her up the stairs and down the hall full of people, not caring if they get kicked by one of her strappy heels as we go by.

"Dude, where you going with her?" one guy asks. He's got on a football jersey and is as tall as I am. He's even wider with all his muscle.

"I'm her security," I growl.

He looks like he's going to argue, and I gotta admire that he cares.

"Come outside with me," I say, "and I'll introduce you to the rest of our team."

Still not taking my word for it, he follows me out.

Jaxon's climbing out of his car and he marches up to Terrence, gesticulating angrily. Then he sees me approaching with Olivia and the anger bleeds out of him, transforming to worry.

"Is she okay? What the fuck—who did this to her?"

"I knocked out an asshole in the basement," I say to Terrence. "Call the police, get him into custody."

Terrence is on it, speaking into his mic to get some other team members to back him up.

"Who the fuck is this guy?" Jaxon asks, pointing to the kid who followed me out of the house.

"Concerned citizen," I say, turning to him. "You convinced yet?"

"Yeah, man. Just wanted to make sure." He spins around to leave.

"Hey," I say.

"Yeah?"

"Get a card from Terrence. Our team can use guys like you, guys who care."

The kid nods and trots off in Terrence's wake.

Now there's only Olivia. I look down at her in my arms. She's closed her eyes, but she isn't asleep.

"Drugged," I say to Jaxon. "I don't know with what."

He drives us to the ER, and I sit in the back seat of his car, holding her against my chest, murmuring things to her that Jaxon can't hear and she'll never remember, anyway.

I can't stand this. She's so insubstantial in my arms. The light of her soul has been diminished by these drugs, by the asshole who attacked her. What would have happened if I hadn't gotten there in time? I want to tear that asshole apart, limb by limb. I've never been so livid, felt so violent, in my entire life, and I don't know what's wrong with me now.

What if we'd lost her? Or if something worse happened to her? I think she'll be okay, probably. Her breathing is even, although shallow.

But this could've gone another way—and that thought infuriates me.

She lifts her hand and presses it to my throat. "You got me," she whispers, her eyes still closed.

She probably thinks I'm Jaxon. That's okay, as long as she feels safe.

So I respond, "Yeah, Babydoll. I got you."

My throat twists at the words and they come out thicker than I intended. I don't want to feel things. Shit. I tamp the feelings down. I'm just offering a service. We're in the bodyguard business, after all.

Her hand falls from my neck and back to her chest where she's curled against me. Still in a whisper, she says, "You're not bad, Ryder."

My heart stops and turns into an anchor in my fucking chest, dropping down. Shit.

"Shows what you know," I say. "You're on drugs right now."

"You can pretend I never said it," she says, "but I'll remember."

~

Jaxon

Olivia stays in the hospital overnight. A woman who looks familiar shows up in the morning and marches straight to the nurse's station near the waiting room where Ryder and I have been hanging out.

"I'm here to see Olivia Santiago," she says in a clear, authoritative voice.

Ryder nudges me. "The mom."

I give the woman a closer look. Her face is heavily made up despite the early hour. Dark circles shadow her eyes, but her silver-blond hair is held back in a tight bun.

I ask Ryder, "Where do I know her from?"

"She's Congresswoman Blankenship."

"Different last name," I say. I'm annoyed, like I should have known who Olivia's mother is, especially if she's a public figure. But I never thought to ask, and Olivia never exactly volunteered the information. When she'd mentioned once that her mother was in politics, I'd just assumed she had a role on the City Council or something like that.

Blankenship is heading straight for us, so we stand up and face her.

Blankenship's gaze is directly on us as she says, "The nurse said you two brought her in?"

"Yes," I say, holding out a hand. "I'm Jaxon Marsel, and this is Ryder Callihan."

She shakes my hand firmly, and then Ryder's. "Why was I only informed she was here this morning?"

"I didn't have your contact information," I say. Blankenship was only called once Olivia woke up and could provide the nurse with her mother's phone number.

"And how do you know my daughter?"

"We're her roommates," I say smoothly. I don't know how much, if anything, Olivia might have shared with her mother about how close we are.

Her appraising glance might intimidate people in her political sphere, but it isn't enough to make me quake. "I see."

Without another word, she turns and strides down the hall.

"Nice first impression," Ryder says with a smirk.

Ignoring the jab, I say, "We should be down the hall with Olivia, too."

Ryder doesn't say anything. Still being a stubborn asshole.

"I'm having a hard time believing the guy who drugged her wasn't her ex," I say.

"I'd bet our entire company that they're connected."

I nod. "Yep. Has anyone seen him since the break-up?"

I wait for Ryder to make some snarky remark about how the night of their break-up was the same night that we'd made her come in the middle of a crowded club, but he only shakes his head.

"No, the asshole seems to have disappeared. Your detective buddy hasn't seen him, either, despite sending officers to check out his apartment three times."

It isn't that difficult to disappear in a city as big as San Esteban, but I'm still annoyed.

Olivia's mom click-clacks down the hallway, coming toward us in her sensible heels and power suit. "I'm expected in the office in twenty-five minutes," she says. "As you two are her...roommates, perhaps you'd be willing to give her a ride home when she's discharged?"

"Of course," I say. "Did the doctor know when that might be?"

"As soon as they can get her paperwork together," she says. "Thank you. She asked to see you, Jaxon."

I nod and thank her, and she hurries off. "Come on," I say to Ryder.

He shakes his head. "I'll be at the office, trying to hunt down this asshole and find out how this happened last night. Because it's *never* happening again."

My thoughts exactly.

~

Olivia

When we come home from the hospital, Jaxon all but carries me up to his penthouse. It's sweet, but I don't need quite that much coddling. My head hurts like hell and I don't feel like I'll ever get enough water in me to quench my thirst, but otherwise I'm fine.

He leads me to the couch and tells me to sit. I squint at him until he lowers his voice and says it a second time. *Yes, Daddy*, I think, feeling the familiar tingling in my lower belly, but all that happens after I sit down is he drags the blanket from the back of the couch and puts it over my legs.

"What are you doing?" I ask.

"Taking care of you."

"I'm not a child," I say, realizing that my tone of voice

makes me sound just like that—a petulant little kid. "Really, Jaxon. I'm okay. Better than okay. I asked them to run some tests...to check for STDs. I'm clean."

"I'm glad to hear that," he says.

"How about you?" I ask, feeling shy all of a sudden. "Have you been tested?"

"I'm clean, too. I can show you the reports if you want. But listen, please." He kneels next to the couch so our faces are level. "I was so fucking scared, Olivia. I've never been more scared of anything in my life. Please, let me take care of you. It is literally the only thing I can think to do right now that will keep me from losing my mind."

"Okay." Tenderness washes through me. I'd been too out of it to be scared of anything last night, but I can imagine what it would feel like to worry about someone I care about.

"Good girl." He stands up. "I'm going to get your e-reader and a snack, and your job is to relax."

"But my final project—"

"Can wait for a day."

The stern tone of his voice triggers my submission. "Got it."

He brings me my e-reader and a bowl of raspberries, then he sits down on the other edge of the couch and puts my feet in his lap.

"Aren't you going to work?" I ask.

"No."

I set down the e-reader. "Why not?"

"I took the day off."

"For...for me?"

He nods. "There's more to my role as your daddy than just spanking, Olivia. You know that, right?"

"I didn't know that until now," I whisper. Our relationship is suddenly very heavy and very real.

"Well, now you know."

Now I know. But I'm in so much trouble.

Because I'm falling for this beautiful, kinky man and he is so far out of my league.

5

———

Olivia

After my day of resting, Jaxon lets me get back into my regular schedule. I don't remember much from the night they found me at the party, other than I do not recognize the guy they found in the basement with me. The thought makes me feel icky inside, and I have a newfound appreciation for Terrence and the other members of the security team. I don't know what made Jaxon guess I needed bodyguards, but I'm so glad he followed his gut.

Two bodyguards are following me at a respectful distance across campus on Thursday afternoon, far enough away that other students don't gawk at me. I'm sure by now some students have guessed that the guys are with me, but in their jeans and black t-shirts, they don't stand out too terribly much, and the campus is large enough that they don't draw a lot of attention.

My phone buzzes in my bag and I fish it out to look at the screen. *Mom.*

I answer, because although we've exchanged a few texts since the hospital, we haven't spoken.

"Olivia," she says, her voice warm. "How are you?"

"I'm good," I say. "The sun is out, I'm wearing a new skirt, and I'm about to put the final touches on my project."

"That's great."

She doesn't even say how she thinks I'm getting a useless degree. Win!

"How are you?" I ask.

We chit-chat for a few minutes, and she tells me about a bill she's trying to gather support for, and I talk about school. I avoid the topic of last weekend, but then she brings it up.

"I wanted to discuss the attack," she says, "and what you're doing to protect yourself."

"Well, I'm not going to any more parties, that's for sure." I've reached the Cassiopeia building, and I yank open the doors, annoyed that Mom's and my nice chat is taking an unhappy turn.

"Good. Are you pressing charges on the man who drugged you?"

"I am, but the police don't think the charges will stick. He insists he found me like that. The door could've been locked from the outside, which is what he says happened."

Mom lets out a growl of frustration. "It's always like this, isn't it? I'm working on a bill with some colleagues that will address the sexism of this system."

"Thanks, Mom," I say. "Look, I just reached my studio. Talk later?"

"Not so fast, young lady," she says with a laugh. "There was one more thing. Your roommates."

I pause with my key in the lock of my studio space. I'm not going into my studio—my happy place—when my mother could turn this into an argument. "What about them?"

"When you first told me you had two guy roommates, I was picturing men your own age. College students. I envisioned t-shirts and cargo shorts with pizza stains."

I laugh because her assumptions were so far from reality, but I do feel bad for not explaining more. "Sorry about that. Jaxon really came through for me after Daniel trashed my apartment. He has a nice place in Midtown."

"And Ryder lives there, too? Are they a couple?"

"No, Ryder has his own place, but he stays there a lot. They're business partners."

"Okay, that makes more sense," she says.

"What makes more sense?" I wonder how much Terrence and Squid can overhear from their position a few yards down the hall.

"Well," she says, "it seemed to me that they are both very much in love with you."

My jaw drops and it takes me a second to recover. "What? You didn't even see them in the room with me."

"The way they talked about you, that's all," she says.

"Mom, you're imagining things." Especially Ryder. Maybe if she'd said Jaxon was in love with me, my pitiful heart would believe, just because the hope of that was so tantalizing. But there was no way she could be reading any of it correctly if she thought Ryder loved me, too.

"Anyway," she says breezily, "I'll let you get to work. But I suspect you're going to have a tough choice to make between those two."

I sigh. "Love you, Mom."

"Love you too, Olivia."

I drop my phone back in my bag and open my studio door.

Before I finish screaming, Terrence and Squid are pulling me aside, trying to keep me from danger.

Nothing can keep me from what I just saw.

Jaxon

When my phone rings with a call from Terrence, I drop my tablet on my desk in my haste to answer. He's on an Olivia shift.

"What is it?" I have to choke out the words, because it turns out, I forgot how to breathe.

At the first notion of anything dangerous to do with Olivia, I turn into a wreck. It surprises me every time, but the truth of the matter is, I care about her so damn much, it makes my body ache. My urge to protect her, to make her happy, to be a positive force in her life—it's all-consuming. I don't understand this because I've never felt this way before, but I can definitely admit to myself that as torturous as it is? I wouldn't change it for one fucking thing.

"Olivia's safe," Terrence begins.

My lungs start working again. Terrence is a good man, telling me immediately. He knows I'm invested in her.

Well, obviously he knows, as she's living with me. Then again, I've never before felt this way about a woman. There's so much more to it.

"What's going on?" I ask.

He says, "More vandalism, this time to her studio. It's...bad. Her sculptures are destroyed."

Her sculptures—fuck. She's an artist. Her ex destroyed a part of her—and what's worse, he's definitely escalating things. And Olivia's going to be devastated. I start to lock my computer and head for the door. I have to be there for her. I have to fix this.

"Where are you?" I ask Terrence. "Are you still there?"

"I'm walking her to the campus police station to make a report."

"Let me talk to her." I wait a second for him to pass the phone, and then say, "Olivia?"

"I'm here."

Her voice is faint and thin, like it could be ripped away in a strong wind. My heart feels like someone ground it to dust in my chest. I hate that she's hurting.

Clearing my throat so that it isn't rough with the emotions I'm feeling, I say, "We're going to find him, okay? We're going to figure this out."

"We can't bring back my art." There's nothing petulant about her tone; she just sounds dull and matter-of-fact.

Despair. That's what I'm hearing in her lack of tone, the lack of her usual Olivia light that shines so bright and pure.

"I know we can't, Babydoll," I say, my chest aching because I need to fix everything and make her feel better, but I can't do that right now. I'll have to drive to campus, and it'll take at least ten minutes. "I don't know if Terrence told you, but I had them install some motion sensor cameras."

"Okay."

"Don't worry, nobody was watching you while you were in your studio working. Footage gets deleted every forty-eight hours and nobody viewed it because nothing happened. But now that something has happened, we'll take a look, and we'll have evidence against whoever did this."

"Evidence against Daniel, you mean."

"Probably him, yes."

She doesn't respond.

"You still there, Babydoll?"

"Yeah. We just reached the police."

"Do you want me to come?" I ask.

"No," she says. "I can handle it."

I'm tempted to go to her anyway, but if I stay here, I can arrange for the footage to be viewed, and for my people to look into this. So I tell her, "If you change your mind, call me and I'll be right there."

"Okay. Thanks."

The call ends and I shout a series of curses at the city beyond my office windows. San Esteban remains silent; it's a city that won't answer back. This is a cruel place, housing the kind of monster who would hurt Olivia so horribly.

Once I catch my breath, I phone Ryder.

"Yeah?" he says.

"Olivia's situation is escalating."

He knows immediately that I'm not talking about my relationship with her. His voice is sharp. "Is she okay?"

"Fuck, I don't think so. Physically yeah, she's fine. Emotionally? She's a wreck. But in a quiet way—I don't know how to talk to her. She was so fucking withdrawn, Ryder, you should've heard her on the phone."

"I'm rushing through three more applications for bodyguards—two of them women with military experience."

That's Ryder—like me, he's got to be moving, taking action, fixing the problem. It's why we make such good business partners.

"Good," I say. Last week, I emphasized we should be recruiting more female guards, anyway, as they're often able to get into places that our male guards can't. They're also better at blending in with civilians.

Ryder speaks again. "Is it bad this time?"

"He ruined her art."

"Motherfucker." Clicking sounds come through the phone, like he's at work on the computer.

"I want guards on her at all hours," I say.

"Already on it."

Olivia

I'm grateful for Terrence's solid presence next to me as I explain to the campus police what happened. The other guard, Squid, stands outside. After I give my report to the officer, Terrence says he'd like a word with the officer privately. Probably to discuss whatever footage they might have of Daniel destroying my work.

All of my art. Gone. I've been working on this project

since last summer. And now it's reduced to ceramic shards. It feels as if someone's scooped out my insides and dropped them on a busy freeway.

Terrence says he needs a word with the campus police officers, so I leave the station and stand next to Squid. With his red hair and pale complexion, Squid is almost the opposite of Terrence, who has brown skin and black hair.

Squid is quiet at first, then clears his throat. "I'm sorry about what happened to your art, Ms. Santiago."

"Thanks," I say through a throat that feels too tight to make a sound.

He doesn't say anything else, but somehow, when my eyes fill with tears, he's ready with a tissue. I take it and wipe my face and nose, then I inhale deeply and straighten my shoulders.

Terrence comes out of the building a few minutes later, his grim mouth framed by his goatee. The guards exchange a look, but I don't even bother trying to decipher it. I'm too tired.

"I'm sorry about what happened today," Terrence says, sounding almost as uncomfortable as Squid.

"I appreciate it." My voice is low, and it sounds like it's coming from somewhere beyond me, or no, that I'm floating somewhere far away from it.

Feeling scraped apart, hollowed out, I realize I can't be on this campus. No good work will come out of today. I'm most creative when I'm happy and in my routine. The whole tortured artist thing has never worked for me.

"I'm going home now," I say.

Home. Jaxon won't be there, which sucks, but at least

I'll be alone, no longer surrounded by the pitying looks of my guards.

It doesn't take us long to get there, and the drive and the parking garage are a blur. As the elevator rises to the penthouse, Terrence asks, "Are you going to be all right, Ms. Santiago?"

Trying not to sniffle, I say, "I'll be fine, thank you."

"We can go inside with you," Squid offers.

I shake my head. I don't want to let anyone see me cry any more than they already have.

"Can we call Mr. Marsel or Mr. Callihan?" Terrence asks. "I'm sure one of them will be here in moments if you need either of them."

Giving him an evaluating look, I frown. I don't know what he thinks he knows, but Ryder Callihan would hardly drop anything to be at my side.

I have a faint dream of Ryder from that night of the party. He was kind in it—more than kind. But I know now that it was a drug-induced fever dream, because the real Ryder is *nothing* like the guy I dreamed.

As soon as I step into Jaxon's penthouse and the elevator doors close behind me, I really let the tears out. Damn Daniel and whatever twisted things are going through his mind. I wonder how I missed the warning signs that he was unhinged, but the more I think back to our relationship, the more I can see them. He alienated all of my friends, one by one. I'd even stopped reaching out to Samantha there, toward the end, and she stuck by me through sheer force of willpower, texting and calling me at least once a day, whether or not I responded.

He never hurt me, although there'd been a side to

him sometimes, especially when he'd been drinking, that made me uneasy.

Thinking about him has made the tears stop, because now instead of crushed, I'm pissed. I wish I could find his stupid phone—the only thing he ever seemed to love—and crush it into tiny pieces in front of his face.

But it wouldn't be enough, because phones are replaceable. My sculpture was the only one of its kind.

Fuck him. Fuck him and his fucking fuck face.

I walk down the hall past the living room and into my bedroom, not Jaxon's. The space smells a little bit like Jaxon from the time he's spent in here with me, but it also smells like Ryder and I don't want to think about why I like that.

Sliding under the covers, I pull them up over my head and blink into the darkness. It will be hours until Jaxon gets off work. Ryder, too. Plenty of time to wallow.

My eyes have barely fallen shut when an awareness tugs me awake again. Footsteps are coming down the hallway, and Jaxon's voice calls out, "Babydoll?"

I sit up to let him know where I am. Both he and Ryder are standing in my bedroom doorway, looks of concern on their faces.

6

———

Jaxon

The lost expression on Olivia's face kills me.

Her gray eyes look like the sky just before it rains, and they're puffy like she's been crying. I rush toward the bed to hold her. Ryder hovers in the doorway. As I take Olivia in my arms, I shoot him a look and mouth, *Get in here.*

He gives a single shake of his head. Fucker doesn't know what's good for him, what's good for Olivia. She likes me, but she likes him, too. I feel the way her body responds when he's around.

She needs us both.

The sooner he sees that, the better for Olivia—and for him.

Olivia sits rigidly in my arms. I can't imagine what she's going through. Her art is her life. She lights up every time she talks about it. I hate that asshole so much for what he's done to her.

"We're going to find him," I murmur into her hair.

"And he's going to pay," Ryder adds.

Olivia nods, but she doesn't say anything. Fuck, I want to make this better, but I don't know how.

Ryder waves a hand, trying to get my attention. I look at him. "What?"

Fuck her, he mouths.

I shake my head. I'm not going to be an asshole. Sex is magic, but it doesn't solve every hurt or every problem in the world.

Shrugging, he walks away.

"Olivia, Babydoll," I murmur into her hair, "what do you need?"

She takes a deep, shuddering breath. "I just want you to hold me. All day. All night."

"I can do that."

"I want to wear my pajamas and be comfortable and not think about what just happened to my project or what it means."

"I'll do whatever it takes to help you with that."

Sitting back, she turns that gray gaze on me. "Will you?"

"I promise, Babydoll." I move to get off the bed, and she frowns. "I'm only getting up to grab your pjs, sweetheart."

"I guess that's all right."

I open her drawer and find a cute little tank top and short set, so I return to the bed, carrying it with me. "Up you go."

She allows me to help her out of bed and out of her clothes, stepping out of her jeans and underwear when I strip them off, lifting her arms so I can tug her shirt over her head. She isn't wearing a bra. Fuck, just the sight of her sweet tits has me hard in my pants. But I restrain myself, and instead of flipping her around and fucking her against the wall like I really want to do, I get the tank top and shorts and dress her.

"Thank you, Daddy," she whispers as I help her back into bed.

I strip out of my dress shirt and slacks so I'm in my boxer briefs and an undershirt.

"Shirt off, Daddy," she says.

I comply and climb into bed next to her, tugging her against me. "Ah, Babydoll. Anything you want. Anything. I'm here for you."

She shakes as she cries in my arms, and I hold her tight until the shaking stops and she's asleep. And I continue to hold her, because that's what she asked for.

I've fallen so fucking hard for this girl. It's exactly what Ryder feared.

I wonder if she knows just how much power she holds in this relationship.

Olivia

I wake up in Jaxon's arms, my cheek resting on his chest. It's dark, but not midnight dark. I can hear Ryder moving around in the next room, maybe getting ready for bed, the TV on quiet.

From Jaxon's breathing, I guess he isn't asleep.

"Hey," I whisper.

"Hey, Olivia."

I slide my hand over his bare chest, loving the feel of his muscles. He flexes his six-pack for me, and I smile. I trail a finger over the ripples of his muscles, then get distracted by his happy trail and start to follow it down to the waistband of his boxer briefs.

"You're giving me ideas," he says in a gruff voice.

"Good," I say.

I know that my art is destroyed, that Daniel's out there maybe plotting another way to ruin my life. But I don't want to think about those things right now. I want to forget it for a little while. I want Jaxon to show me that I can feel joy in his arms, that the world isn't a terrible place all the time.

He captures my wrist before I can delve into his underwear and grab his cock. I pout at him, and he touches my lip. Flicking out my tongue, I taste the pad of his thumb.

His dark eyes grow even darker and he turns onto his side to face me fully. "What do you think you're doing?"

"Tasting you." I send out my tongue and lick the tip of his thumb like I'd do to his cock. "You taste yummy, Daddy."

"Fuck, Babydoll."

He turns me over so I'm on all fours and tugs my hips into the air. His palm is against my pussy immediately, cupping me through my sleep shorts. The heat of his hand gets me wriggling. I want more of that contact, more of that heat.

Removing his hand from my pussy, he yanks my shorts down. Cool air hits my ass and pussy lips. He bends down to me and I feel his lips on my ass, then his teeth as he bites me gently.

"Do you want us to use a condom?" he asks.

"No. You said you're clean. And I am. I have an IUD, too."

"That's great," he says. "I can't wait to slide into you, nothing between us."

"Me, too," I whisper.

I try to move my knees to get the sleep shorts out of the way, but he says, "No. Leave them."

He's up and leaning over me again, his cock head at my entrance, then moving past it, running through my slick arousal.

"I love playing in your wetness," he says gruffly. "I love knowing how ready you are for me."

"Mmm," I moan.

"What was that, Babydoll?" he asks sharply.

Just then, the sounds of the television in Ryder's room go off.

I whisper, "I like it, too."

"What do you like?" he asks, not bothering to keep his voice down.

"I like you playing in my wetness," I say quietly.

He smacks my ass. "I can't hear you. Speak up."

My face burns. Ryder shouldn't have to listen to all of this. But Jaxon rubs his hand over the stinging globe of my ass, and I know he'd be all too happy to spank me again.

A little louder, I say, "I like you playing in my wetness."

"That's a good girl," he says, then slides into my pussy.

I gasp at the fullness of him there. So good. So thick. It's different without the condom. Warmer, I think. He slides in easily and then holds still, probably because he knows it drives me mad with need to feel him there, not moving, showing me how much control he has over my body.

"Ah, I can just stay here forever," he says.

He brings a hand to my hair and wraps my ponytail around it, getting a good grip before he yanks my head back.

"Play with your tits," he says, his voice gruff.

I brace myself on one arm and use my other to play with one nipple, then the other. My hands are too small to reach both at once. As I tweak them alternately, my pussy squeezes down, too, clamping on Jaxon's cock. I need him to start thrusting, but I know better than to try rocking back to force the movement.

He lets go of my hair and reaches past me for the nightstand. He pulls out a bottle of lube. Sucking in a breath, I try to keep myself from moaning. I know what he's going to do next.

"Oh, beautiful girl," he says as he dribbles lube down the crack of my ass, "this is going to feel so good for you."

"Mmmff," is all I can say as I bury my face in the pillow.

When he starts trailing his fingers over the lube in my crack, I automatically jerk away from the strange sensation.

"Come back here, doll." He holds my hip with one hand and circles my anus with his other thumb. "You're so tight here. Let Daddy take care of you, okay?"

I know he isn't really asking me if it's okay. Still, I turn my head back so I can see him out of the corner of my eye. His eyes are heavy-lidded with lust, his brow furrowed with concentration. When he sees me looking at him, he grins, his teeth looking even whiter in the dim light of the room.

"I like that eye contact," he says. "Keep looking at me."

My eyes want to flutter shut when he presses his thumb into my ass, but I want so badly to please him, I keep them open through sheer force of will. He thrusts his cock a few times into my pussy as a reward, and a moan tears itself from my lips.

"I love those sounds," Jaxon says, thrusting again and moving his thumb in my ass while he does it. He leans forward and his breath is hot against my ear when he says, "You know he's listening to us right now, don't you, you dirty girl?"

Yes, I'm aware of Ryder in the other room, close enough to hear all of this. My pussy spasms around Jaxon's cock.

"That's right, Babydoll," he says in a loud voice, "you love my thumb in your ass, don't you? I'll be fucking you there someday soon."

I can't believe he's being so loud. He's *trying* to let Ryder hear.

"Shh," I say.

"Don't be shy," Jaxon says, then thrusts so hard into me, I can't help but cry out again.

"Please," I whisper. "I don't want—"

Whatever I was going to say next is forgotten when he thrusts again. He reaches around me with his free hand to grab one of my breasts and pinches the nipple roughly. A spark of pure ecstasy shoots through my body, straight to my clit, and an orgasm rocks through my body. I moan through it, trying to keep my voice down.

"That's right, sweetheart," Jaxon says, none too quietly. "Come for Daddy."

"Fuck," Ryder says in the next room.

I freeze and whisper, "We woke him up."

"No, Babydoll, I can guarantee he's been listening this whole time."

He pumps into me again and again, and I feel another orgasm beginning.

7

———

Ryder

Listening to Olivia come is exquisite torture. I want to go in there and watch more than anything. Jaxon wouldn't give a fuck—he'd like it. Olivia might like it, too, the same way she liked it when I watched them in the living room. But it's something we should talk about before we do it, not something I should surprise her with while Jaxon's comforting her.

And he's comforting her exactly the way I told him to, the bastard. I knew it was what she needed.

"Daddy," she whimpers.

"Your pussy's squeezing my cock so good, Babydoll," he says. "Don't move your hips. I'll give you what you want."

There's another whimper from Olivia. Then a sharp *smack*.

"I told you to hold still, Babydoll. You'll get it when I give it to you, don't be greedy." Jaxon's voice is a croon, but there's an edge to it. From Olivia's responding moan, that works for her.

"We shouldn't be so loud," she says. "This is embarrassing."

"Really?" He sounds amused. "Hey, Ryder, can you come here for a second?"

Dammit. I can't say I'm surprised, but this is a bad idea.

"No," Olivia moans, drawing out the word.

"Is that your safeword, Olivia?" he asks.

I can picture her cute little scowl as she says in a sulky voice, "You know it isn't."

Permission enough for me. I saunter down the hall and knock on the door frame to her room. "You wanted something, Jaxon?"

I stand straight and try to keep a disinterested face, as if the scene before me isn't the hottest fucking thing I've ever witnessed. Olivia's on all fours, her head buried in a pillow—probably because she's embarrassed. Jaxon kneels behind her with his hand splayed on her ass—thumb in her hole, from the looks of it and from what he'd been so loudly saying a few minutes ago.

"Yeah," Jaxon says, slowly thrusting in and out of Olivia. "Babydoll here is worried that we're being too loud for you. Are we disturbing you?"

I glare at him. He's flaunting what he has—the most beautiful girl in the world splayed out in front of him, her ass and pussy filled with his fingers and cock. The arch of her spine is delicate, sexy. Her brown locks, tumbling over the pillow, speak of passion and lust.

My dick is rigid in my sweatpants, which anyone

looking can clearly see. Thankfully, Olivia's hiding her face.

"You're not disturbing me at all," I say lightly. "Except for asking me to come in here."

"Did you hear that, Olivia?" Jaxon asks, giving her ass a swat.

"Yes," she mumbles.

"Look at Mr. Ryder when you speak, and tell him you're sorry that we had to call him in here."

"Jaxon," she whines. "Please."

He smacks her ass again, and she raises her head. Her cheeks are pink, her gray eyes are wide. They get wider when she notices my boner. She whispers, "I'm sorry we had to call you in here."

"You'll call him *Sir* or *Mr. Ryder*," Jaxon tells her.

"I'm sorry, Sir," she says.

And the words go straight to my cock. It feels heavier than a fucking crowbar in my sweats.

"Yeah," I say, "no problem."

Jaxon resumes fucking her, slow strokes that flex his ass and shake her tits, and Olivia hides her face again.

He locks his gaze on me. "What's your problem?" he asks, then leans forward and takes one of Olivia's perfect tits in his hand.

"No problem at all," I say. "Goodnight."

I go back to my room and listen to the two of them going at it for hours. I could rub one out to the sounds of Olivia's hoarse cries and moans, but instead I lie still on my bed, picturing everything they're doing.

～

Olivia

The next morning, Ryder isn't around when Jaxon and I get up. Jaxon laughs when he hears my relieved sigh.

"You know, he'd join in with us if he wasn't so stubborn," Jaxon says.

"What?" I take a sip of the smoothie he hands me. "He would not. And besides…I'm yours, right?"

The pleased look on his face warms me all the way through. "You are mine, Olivia. That's exactly right. But Ryder fascinates you. He turns you on. You came on his fingers at the club, the night we first met."

"I—well…" My face heats and I try to hide it.

He gives a rumbling growl of satisfaction. "Get on your knees, Babydoll."

I scurry to do as he asked. The kitchen tiles are cold. Seeing me wince, Jaxon grabs a towel that was hanging near the sink and tosses it to the floor.

Scooting forward, I find a comfortable position on the towel. "Thank you, Daddy."

"Take out my cock, Olivia."

I carefully pull down his black sweatpants, revealing a semi-hard cock right in front of my face.

"Now put me in your mouth, let me feel your throat."

The head of his cock is smooth and hard against my tongue. His pre-come is tangy and I salivate, then swallow so I don't drool.

"Fuck," he says. "Your mouth feels so good. Suck me off and play with yourself, Babydoll. Show me how much my cock turns you on."

I work my mouth over him, sucking and licking,

holding the base of him in my fist for the angles I want. Slurping sounds fill the kitchen area, obscenely loud.

"Don't forget to touch yourself," he says.

Keeping one hand on his cock, I bring the other one to the apex of my legs and touch myself through my sleep shorts.

"So I want to tell you something, Olivia," Jaxon says as I suck him.

"Mm-hmm?" I say around his dick. I dip my hand beneath the waistband of my sleep shorts and rub my fingers over my pussy. I'm so wet, so wanton.

"Sometimes babydolls have more than one daddy to take care of them."

I freeze and look up at his face, trying to gauge his seriousness.

"Nice eye contact, Olivia," he says, stroking my cheek. "Keep sucking."

I do as he asks. The rigid length of him keeps me grounded to this moment, this place, him. Everything is Jaxon right now—Jaxon and me, together.

He continues, "More than one daddy means a babydoll's beautiful, greedy little cunt can be filled by more than one cock. Or she gets to suck on one daddy's cock while the other daddy fucks her pussy or her sweet little asshole."

His filthy words fill my mind, sparking new, forbidden images. My fingers fly over my pussy, focusing on my clit.

"Don't come, Olivia," he says. "Don't fucking come. Play with your nipples now."

I whimper and pull my hand from my shorts to do as he asks, sliding my hand beneath my top. My fingers are sticky-slippery over my breasts as I squeeze first one, then the other, focusing on the hard, aroused peaks of my nipples.

"I think you'd like to have a second daddy." Jaxon wraps my hair around one of his hands and holds my head in place. "Relax your jaw, Babydoll. This is going to be rough. Just for a minute. If you want to use your safeword, hit my leg."

Relaxing my jaw, I'm taken completely by his rapid thrusting. My eyes water. I struggle to breathe through my nose. A second later, he growls, "Olivia."

Then he's emptying down my throat and I swallow his come. Even though the orgasm was all his, I feel complete in another way. Powerful.

He pulls away from my mouth, then reaches for my arms and lifts me up. "Good girl. You deserve a reward. What do you want?"

"I want to come," I say, looking at him through my eyelashes.

"Step out of your sleep shorts and show me your beautiful cunt."

I do as he asks. His fingers are against me immediately, slick with my arousal, and he pumps them inside.

"Jaxon," I gasp. "Daddy. I need to come."

"Yes, Babydoll. You can come on my fingers." He does something, changes the angle somehow, and it feels even more amazing.

"That—whatever you're doing—yes," I gasp.

"I want you to think about another man behind you, working your ass while I work your pussy."

The fantasy that plays in my mind isn't of just any man. It's Ryder standing behind me, like he was at the club. Only now it's my ass, not my pussy, that he touches.

In my wicked fantasy, Ryder is thrusting his cock into my back hole while Jaxon fingers me.

"Oh," I moan, as the ecstasy intensifies in my lower body.

Jaxon lowers his head and sucks on one of my nipples through the fabric of my top. His mouth is scorching and the suction so strong that it stings. The pain and pleasure twine together, sending electricity straight to my clit, which he flicks with his thumb while his fingers thrust inside of me.

My orgasm is sudden and strong, and I collapse against him.

"Eye contact, Babydoll," Jaxon says.

I lift my head from his chest and open my eyes. His handsome face should be immortalized somewhere, with those strong cheekbones, his neat beard that highlights the shape of his jaw, and those bedroom eyes, dark and penetrating.

Jaxon licks his fingers clean, his gaze never leaving mine.

"One question for you, Olivia," he says.

"Okay."

"Who did you think of, when I told you to picture another man behind you?"

I try to look away, but he nudges my chin back toward him.

My face feels hot. I'd thought my fantasy was private. "I don't want to say."

"But I'd really like to hear it," he says.

"It doesn't matter, though."

"No?" He tugs me closer, then lifts me in an embrace

before carrying me to the couch, where he sits with me in his lap.

Automatically, I snuggle my head against his chest and the crook of his neck. I'm grateful that from this position, I can't make eye contact with him.

His voice is an even deeper rumble when I listen to it through his chest. "If it doesn't matter, you should say it."

He's not going to let this go. And maybe I don't want him to.

"Ryder," I admit. "I thought of Ryder."

"Good girl." His hand travels to my bare pussy and he plays there again until I'm panting and writhing in his lap.

8

Olivia

There's a new bodyguard working with Terrence —a woman, this time. Lisa. Jaxon's trying to hire more women, apparently. Lisa seems cool like Terrence, for the most part, but there's something about the way she looks at me with her very pale green eyes that makes me feel weird. She and Terrence follow me around campus, my ever-present shadows. They sit near my table, but not too near, when I have coffee with Samantha.

"It has been *way* too long," Samantha says while we sip on our drinks.

We're each indulging in the sweetest, fanciest offerings of the café. My "coffee" even has a dollop of whipped cream and rainbow sprinkles. It makes me feel like a little girl, which reminds me of how I've been spending my time with Jaxon. My daddy. It sounds so twisted, and yet...so perfect.

"Yeah, you need to either tell me about that goofy grin on your face," Samantha says, "or you need to make it go away. Because whatever you're having? That's what *I* want."

I laugh. I haven't told Samantha everything about Jaxon's kink—and my newfound kink. I will eventually, but for now, it's still new and I want to think about it on my own for a while longer before bringing it out into the light for others to consider. "Jaxon's just really great, that's all."

"That is not all," she says, but she's smiling and her bright blue eyes are sparkling. "I'm glad you're happy, Olivia. It's all I could ask for after all the shit Daniel has put you through."

"Let's not talk about him, please." I can't revisit the dark place my mind goes to when I think about what he did to my art. He broke a piece of me and it's going to take time to heal.

"Good call." Samantha takes a sip of her drink. "What's your plan, anyway?"

As much as I don't want to talk about it, I need to let Samantha know what's going on. Taking a deep breath, I say, "I talked to Professor Browning."

She wrinkles her nose. "And what did that hardass have to say?"

"She actually told me to continue as if everything is intact."

"Whoa, really?" Samantha raises her perfectly shaped eyebrows. "Who would've thunk?"

I make myself smile back. "Right? We have photographs I'd been taking to put into the final project notes. So I don't have to create anything new from scratch. But it's just…Sam, you know part of the appeal was the final show. I was supposed to unveil my art. People were going to come and see what I'd done. We'd talk about it. I was nervous as fuck, of course—"

"Oh, I remember," Samantha says with a laugh.

"And now it's just some photos in a cheaply bound report."

"Hey, it's still awesome, what you made," she says, giving my foot a gentle kick with hers.

"Yeah." It's gone now, though, and that's the part that hurts. I don't want to keep going on and on about it, so I keep quiet.

She sighs. "I get it, though. Or I kind of do, anyway. If someone destroyed the novel I've been writing for my final project, I'd probably feel the same. Even if I were to rewrite it, it wouldn't be the exact novel I'd written before."

"Yeah." I inhale, exhale. Again. And try not to cry.

I know there are worse things in the world—hunger, illness, pain, and true loss. So it feels trivial to want to cry about my art.

But damn it—that was a piece of myself, and Daniel destroyed it.

Suddenly, I don't want to talk anymore. I slurp up the rest of my drink, forcing it down a throat that now feels too tight to swallow.

"I should probably get going," I say.

"Sure, babes," Samantha says. The sympathy in her pretty blue eyes nearly makes me cry, but I keep it together. "Catch you later?"

"Yeah, thanks." I give her a swift hug and haul ass out of the coffee shop. Terrence and Lisa aren't far behind me, so I feel safe enough ducking into Cassiopeia to use the restroom. I need to splash some cold water on my face, otherwise everyone will be able to tell I'm holding back tears.

Lisa, the female bodyguard, is right on my heels as I round the corner toward the restrooms. I give her a look, because none of the bodyguards have followed me this closely before.

She follows me all the way into the bathroom, and I'm starting to freak out as I stop in front of one of the sinks. Is it normal for her to stick so close? I haven't had a female bodyguard before, but everything about her is raising my inner alarm.

"Can I get a little space, please?" I ask.

"Sure."

But she's standing right there at the counter, staring at me in the mirror. She's pretty, I realize, with pouty lips and heavy-lidded green eyes that scream *fuck me*. Her generous chest is accentuated by a couple of buttons undone on her blouse.

She smiles at me when she sees me taking her measure. "How's it going, Olivia?"

"Um. Fine." Feeling skittish, I back up into a stall, then lock the door behind me.

"Are you dating them both?" she asks through the door. "Or is Ryder free?"

"What?" I open the stall door to face her, stunned by the question.

She's out of breath from hurrying after me, and now that the door isn't between us, she's very much standing in my personal space. Where the fuck is Terrence?

He's outside, because we're in the ladies room. Of course.

She says, "I was just wondering if Ryder was available, or if you're fucking him *and* Jaxon."

"I don't—I don't—"

"Albertson." Terrence's deep voice comes through the main door to the restroom. "Get your ass out here *now*."

She winks at me as she leaves. "I take it that he's available, then."

After the door closes behind her, I walk over to the sinks and stare into the mirror. My face looks pale and the dark circles under my eyes are more pronounced than ever. When I run the water to splash water on my face, my hands are shaking.

Both of the bodyguards are waiting near the restroom door when I leave. Terrence looks pissed, and I want to ask about what's happening, but Lisa's gleeful expression is too off-putting. I'll ask later. I don't understand her questions. It hardly feels appropriate that she asked about Ryder, but why shouldn't she? Probably her and every other person who likes men would be attracted to Ryder.

It's fine, I tell myself. I'm not sleeping with Ryder and I have no claim on him. Other people are free to pursue him. He's free to sleep with whoever he wants to sleep with.

Even if the very thought of it makes me feel sick.

When I get home, Jaxon isn't there yet. Ryder is in his room, talking on the phone. He sounds agitated, so I stay in the living room to give him privacy, rather than going to my room where it would be much easier to eavesdrop.

Unfortunately, he gets angry enough that he raises his voice.

"She's become a huge fucking problem," he says.

I hope he's not talking about me, but then again, it wouldn't be a surprise. He hasn't exactly made it a secret that he doesn't want me around.

"Yes, it was a fucking mistake. Olivia doesn't deserve this."

I suck in a breath. He *is* talking about me.

The way he says it—angry, unforgiving, yet strangely controlled—hurts more than anything else. His complete disdain for me is summed up in four words. *Olivia doesn't deserve this.* All along, I've known I don't deserve this— any of it. This life, with Jaxon and maybe even with Ryder, is too good to be true. Too good for me.

"Just stop," Ryder says. "It's time to get rid of her already."

Then a moment later, he says, "Glad you agree, Jax."

My hands are trembling. I don't know what I'd hoped. Maybe I'd hoped that Jaxon was right and Ryder would eventually realize he had feelings for me. Maybe I'd hoped that Jaxon was wrong and Ryder would eventually move away and leave the two of us alone so we could be happy without tiptoeing around him.

But I didn't hope for complete and utter rejection.

From both of them. *Glad you agree, Jax.*

And I didn't hope for the truth to be thrown in my face like this. Because Ryder's right—I don't deserve this. I don't know what I could have done to get so lucky. Jaxon noticed me in that club. I wasn't anything special. But he'd singled me out and danced with me, and gotten Ryder to dance with me, too.

In the end, though, I don't deserve that attention or that love.

It's never been clearer to me than it is now—I have overstayed my welcome in Jaxon and Ryder's penthouse.

Ryder

As I end my phone call with Jaxon, I hear soft footsteps in the kitchen. Olivia's here. The heavy feeling in my chest immediately lightens when I think about seeing her. It's strange how quickly my world has reorganized itself around her, how I now try to come home earlier in the hopes of seeing her, talking to her.

I want her to look at me the way she looks at Jaxon. I want her respect, her affection.

I want her submission.

I want to give her the world.

It scares the shit out of me.

Tossing my phone on the bed, I leave the room in search of her. Maybe I'll get us each a beer and we can relax. If I could get her to talk to me a little more, maybe both of us could loosen up.

I find her in the kitchen. She's holding a glass of water with one hand. Her other arm is wrapped around her body, like she's trying to protect herself.

"You okay?" I ask.

"Yep." Her voice is strangely high-pitched, revealing tension.

I come around the kitchen counter and move to the cupboard of glasses to get myself some water—and also to give her a closer examination. Something isn't right.

She turns away from me as I get closer, but not before I get a peek at her expression.

The look on her face troubles me. It's a combination of sorrow and another emotion, something I can't figure out entirely. After her horrible ex ruined her sculptures, I thought I'd seen her in complete despair.

But this is something beyond that. It looks as if she's given up. But on what?

"Hey," I say.

She spins around and disappears down the hallway.

Well, that was weird. And disrespectful. Irritated, I call after her, "Hey, don't walk away from me."

"You're not my daddy," she says from the living room.

Maybe not, but I'm tempted as fuck to spank her ass right now. I'm mad enough that one of our bodyguards screwed up—I'm not about to put up with Olivia's bratty behavior.

Sighing, I pour her a glass of the flavored water she likes so much and return to the living room.

But she's not sitting on one of the couches. I look around, as if she might be hiding behind one. Did she go to Jaxon's room to escape me? My palm itches with the urge to spank her bad attitude away.

A *swish* sound catches my attention—the sound of the elevator closing. Turning, I see the tiny light indicating that it's traveling downward.

Great, now I've driven her away.

Fuck my life. I can't do anything right.

9

———

Jaxon

My potential new client bites her lip as she evaluates me. A musician who has recently come to the media's attention, she's extremely charismatic and knows how to flaunt her attributes.

I'm not interested, though. A month ago, I might have canceled this business arrangement and taken her out for some fun. But now, I have Olivia.

Ashley Jean, the musician, is pouting when I look up again, her lower lip protruding delicately.

"And you're wanting the services of Ironwood Security for what, exactly?" I ask, ignoring the pout. "A special occasion?"

She shrugs. "For anything, really. I want the appearance."

I hold in my sigh. It isn't the first time an up-and-coming celebrity wants the cachet of a security team, without actually needing security. I'm happy to provide it, but, "You realize you could work out a much less pricey contract with any number of private security companies, don't you?"

"Yes," she says, "but I hear you're the best."

"Damn straight Ironwood is the best." I tap my pen on the folder in front of me, then flash my focus to the computer monitor. "Tell you what, Ms. Jean. On the understanding that you are in no real danger, I'll be using your security detail as a way to train up some new members of my team, pairing them with more experienced bodyguards. You will receive a discount with the appearance of having a full-service Ironwood security team, and I will have on-the-job training for new employees. How does that sound?"

"Perfect," she says, standing up and shaking my hand. "Genevieve said you were amazing, and she was totally right."

It takes a moment for her words to completely penetrate my mind, because everything stuttered to a halt on the name *Genevieve*. But I give her a bland smile and see her out of the room.

Surely she can't mean my ex. That can't be right. Genevieve returned to Paris. Ashley had to mean someone else. Unbidden images float through my mind —Genevieve's twisted mouth as she screams that she never wants to see me again. Genevieve's middle finger, jabbing up through the limo's sunroof as she rides to the airport.

No, Ashley was talking about a different Genevieve. Because the Genevieve I know wouldn't have a single kind word to say about me.

The buzzing of my phone reclaims me to the here and now. I glance down to see Ryder's name on the screen, so I swipe to answer.

"What is it?" I ask.

"She's gone," he says. "She took off."

I glance at the clock. It's almost four-thirty, and I've been planning to leave early today, anyway.

"Where would she go?" I ask. She's almost always home by the time I get there, snuggled into the couch and waiting for me. "Tell me she called in Terrence—"

"She did *not* call Terrence. Fuck, Jax, you're not listening to me. She's *gone*. She left. She's not answering her phone."

I want to yell, "What did you do to her," but that won't solve the current problem. Instead I say, "Call Terrence—"

"Already have."

"Arrange a team to search for her."

"Already done."

Raking a hand through my hair, I struggle to hold my temper. "Where are you?" I ask.

"Driving to her friend's house to look for her there. Samantha or something, she lives close to the university. Terrence is on his way to the campus."

"Was she upset when she left?"

"Yes. And no, I don't know why. She looked crushed." He swears. "Did she...shit. She might've overheard me talking to you about Lisa Albertson."

Lisa Albertson—the new security team member who had gone rogue today and followed Olivia into the bathroom. Terrence was pissed about that. I replay the conversation in my head. *It's time to get rid of her.* Did Ryder ever say Albertson's name? I can't recall.

"I'm on my way out," I say.

"Where are you going?"

"I don't fucking know. We have to find her, Ryder."

He sounds just as desperate as I feel as he says, "I know. We will. We fucking will."

Olivia

I should have grabbed some clothes, but I wasn't thinking. I dial Samantha's number again, praying for her to pick up. I need somewhere to stay tonight. She can at least let me sleep on her floor. And then tomorrow, I'll find a place of my own.

Or I could stay with my mom. Ugh. There's a reason our relationship improved one thousand percent after I moved out. In the case of our relationship, absence truly does make the heart grow fonder.

Until I can get in touch with Samantha, I trek to the coffee shop on campus. I get my favorite sugary coffee drink, but it sits in front of me, condensation collecting on the cup, and I don't even take a sip. My stomach is an empty pit and I don't feel like drinking or eating. Whenever I remember Ryder's harsh voice as he spoke of getting rid of me, my eyes fill with tears, so I do my best to stop thinking about it. But really, that's all my brain seems capable of doing. Ryder and Jaxon, Jaxon and Ryder. Their images fill my mind. Not only the erotic moments I shared with Jaxon—and sometimes Ryder, peripherally —but the tender moments, as well.

Dammit. I need to stop thinking. I should've gone for liquor instead of caffeine.

While I've been sitting here, the sun has fallen and twilight has descended over the campus. The Cassiopeia building is just across the lawn, its front steps lit by cheerful lamps along the walk.

Leaving my drink behind, I move on autopilot toward the building. Art has always been my solace, any time I was upset. And Daniel has already destroyed everything there, so he would have no reason to return and destroy more.

There's a chill in the air. It bites through my sweatshirt. I'm starting to feel exposed, walking toward Cassiopeia by myself. Probably because I'm not followed by security for the first time in a long time. But if Jaxon and Ryder want to get rid of me, why would they keep paying someone to watch me? I'm going to have to take some self-defense classes and make sure I only go out during the day or in groups.

Reaching the front door of Cassiopeia gives me a small feeling of safety, because I'm no longer out in the open. I hurry inside and down the hall to my studio. My hand is shaking as I unlock the door, let myself in, and lock it behind me again. I really hope I don't have to sleep here tonight.

My phone rings again, and this time it's Jaxon's name that pops up on the screen instead of Ryder's. Tears well in my eyes, but I blink them back. I can't talk to him right now. It's too raw. Maybe tomorrow, or the next day, or ten years from now, I'll be able to talk to him about what I did wrong, why I'm not right for him.

I can't bear to block his number or Ryder's. And I need to keep my phone on to wait for Samantha to text me back.

My phone stops ringing and a text from Jaxon pops up almost immediately. *Babydoll. Call me.*

I can imagine his authoritative voice speaking the words and I nearly comply. But he isn't my daddy anymore. As soon as he agreed with Ryder that they need to get rid of me, that arrangement ended.

My studio is dark and I consider turning on the lights, but I don't want anyone outside to be able to see me, and the blinds are trashed. Besides, if I'm sitting in the dark, I can't as clearly see the dust and rubble from my crushed sculpture, and that's a blessing in itself. I find a spot on the floor and sit cross-legged, phone next to me on the tile. I'll camp out here until Samantha texts.

The doorknob rattles, and I nearly leap up to hide behind the desk on the other side of the room. But nothing else happens, other than footsteps. Someone probably had the wrong room number.

The door slams open, and someone steps into the room. I stifle my shriek and fall back against the wall. The man looks left, then right, and his gaze locks with mine. His green eyes look meaner than ever as he glares down his pointed nose at me.

Daniel.

"You—you can't be here," I say. "There's a restraining order—"

"Restraining order," he sneers.

"Yes." I try to make my voice sound braver than I actually feel. "I'm giving you one chance to get out of here."

"Do you know how pissed my dad is?" he asks. "I can't go anywhere, do anything. He killed my access to my trust fund, made it so I can't use the car service."

Does he have any idea what a spoiled brat he sounds like? I subtly try to reach for my phone, but Daniel's attention is caught by my movement.

"Not so fast," he says, kicking it away before squatting in front of me so we're eye to eye. "We need to have a nice, long talk."

There's a creepy smile on his face, although his skin is sallow, and dark circles make his eyes look more protuberant than usual.

"You're going to come with me," he says.

As he reaches for me, I reach for him. He looks pleased at first, but I keep reaching until my arms are at his shoulders, then I shove back—hard.

"Bitch," he says.

He falls to his ass and I jump up. I leave my phone behind and spin to go to the door.

A hand clamps on my ankle and the floor rushes toward me. My head bangs into the wall. There isn't even time to scream before everything around me goes dark.

10

———

Jaxon

She's not answering my calls, nor my texts. I don't know where she could be.

I stalk to the café she likes, but it's closed. A lone worker sweeps the floor. I bang on the door until he mouths, "We're closed."

Yes, dumbass, I can tell. I say, "It's an emergency. I just need to ask you a question."

He looks like he wants to flip me off, but he makes the wise choice and answers the door.

"Thank you," I say, holding up my phone to show him a picture of Olivia that I'd snapped the other day so I could see it when she called. "Have you seen this woman?"

"Yeah, she was in here a while ago," he says.

"How long ago?" I ask.

"Hmm, an hour? Maybe two?"

"Did you see where she went after?"

He shakes his head. "Sorry. I hope you find her."

"Thanks," I say, already turning around to go back to my car. Then I see her art building. Would she have gone there? It's the scene of Daniel's destruction, but if she was upset, that might not matter.

The outside door is unlocked. Already unusual. I hurry down the hallway to her studio. The door is open, but the light's off. She wouldn't be in there like this—but she also wouldn't leave the door open.

I step inside, flip on the lights. The room's empty except her crushed sculpture...and her handbag and phone. The phone is clear across the room, and a mark in the dust shows it was slid there, possibly kicked.

Foul play. Her ex found her here, I just know it.

I pick up her handbag and phone, then run to my car while I call Ryder. "I'm leaving her studio. The ex got her."

"I'm close to his apartment, I'll go there now."

Daniel wouldn't have taken her there, but it makes sense to check. "Where else can I look?" I ask.

"Terrence dug up info on him. Daniel only has the apartment. His father's country club would be one place, but his dad revoked his membership after the restraining order."

And here I'd thought it was overkill to have the little asshole investigated. Evidently not. It's helping us narrow down possibilities now.

"Where the fuck else could he have taken her?" I ask. "What other property does his family own?"

"Hang on. I just reached his apartment building. I have the property listings in an email and I'll check as soon as I park."

I wait, gripping my phone so hard I'm surprised it doesn't crack.

"They have a cabin on the lake," Ryder says. "Thirty minutes away."

He rattles off the address and I plug it into my car's GPS.

"Double-check the apartment," I say, "then meet me at the cabin."

"On it."

I jam down the accelerator and speed toward the lake. *I'm coming, Olivia. I'll be there soon.*

~

Olivia

I wake to a thudding sensation in my head. I don't want to open my eyes, especially when I remember what just happened. Whatever I see won't be good.

But even if I keep my eyes closed and pretend this isn't happening, it won't change a damn thing. Daniel will still be here. He's carrying me somewhere, I realize. That jarring feeling is him carrying me. He's bringing me down some stairs, maybe?

I don't struggle yet—I don't want him to know I'm awake. First, I need to figure out where we are. Somewhere on campus? The air is damp, humid. When I squint my eyes open, everything is dark, darker than I'm used to. Are we not in San Esteban anymore?

A bony pressure digs into my gut—he's got me over his shoulder, and I'm staring at his back. Looking down, I can see that we're going *up* stairs, not down them.

I need more information if I'm going to come up with a plan.

"Daniel?" I ask.

"You're awake, good."

"Can you put me down? I feel like I'm going to throw up."

The jarring stops for a moment before he says, "Nah, I don't think so. We're nearly to the second floor."

Everything around me seems to spin around and suddenly my bare feet are on plush, expensive carpet. The area is dark, but I can make out some details.

"Where are we?" I ask.

"My family's cabin. You always wanted to come here, remember?"

"Yes...just not under circumstances like this," I say. It was a point that used to annoy me—I wanted to come to the lake, and he wanted to stay in my apartment and play video games all day.

He laughs, and the queasiness in my stomach returns. I have no weapon. No phone. No way to get help. How will anyone find me out here?

We've reached the top of the stairs.

"Come on, I have a room all set up for you," he says.

"Just...a second," I say, and I don't have to fake my gasps or the nausea. Sweat breaks out over my face. The thought of being trapped here with him physically sickens me.

I flail my arms around until I find the banister and I latch on, leaning over it.

"Don't hurl here," Daniel says. "I don't want to have the carpets cleaned."

His hand comes down hard over my shoulder,

whether as his twisted version of comfort, or as a warning not to puke, I don't know. But the touch seals my resolve —it means he's close enough, and he's between me and the staircase.

I kick out at his knee, putting all my weight into it while holding on tight to the banister.

His mouth opens in a round O of surprise. He teeters on the top stair, then grasps for my arm. Still holding tightly to the banister, I spin and jerk away from his reach, then kick his leg again.

He goes down with a shout and several ugly thuds.

All is quiet. I don't want to look. I don't want to know what happened to him, but I have to know if he's already climbing back up again. My breath comes in shaky gasps as I slowly kneel on the top step and look down.

In the movies, the villain usually lands with an unnatural turn to the neck or limbs, but Daniel looks like he just leaned against the wall next to the lower landing and took a nap. His legs are splayed comically.

I can't tell whether or not his chest is rising and falling. I don't want to have killed him, but I'm terrified at the thought of him jumping up and grabbing me.

I have to go down the stairs to get out of this house. My throat feels tight with fear, but I hurry down. I leap past him, praying he doesn't reach out and grab my leg again. Thankfully, he doesn't budge.

Glancing wildly around, I don't see a landline telephone anywhere. I'm not about to go near Daniel to see if he has his cell with him. It would be safer to run down the road and hope to find a neighbor.

The hardwood floor is smooth against my bare feet as I rush to across the entryway and to the door. What did he do with my shoes? Maybe they fell off in his car. I push the door open and take in great gulps of damp air.

A low moan catches my attention and I turn around. Daniel moves an arm, but he doesn't get up.

I have to get out of here.

There's a pair of rubber boots by the door. I pull them on. They're way too big for me, but the driveway seems endless from this patio, and it's made of gravel. The boots will get me across it without cutting up my feet.

My wish for neighbors is in vain. When I reach the road, it stretches and curves, and I can't see any lights nearby. I have no idea which direction would be the best one to go in. I just want to sink to the asphalt and cry, but that certainly won't save me.

The only thing I can think about is Daniel waking up and chasing after me. I start to run, but the boots nearly trip me, so I yank them off and throw them into the vegetation crowding the side of the road.

Then, barefoot, I begin to run.

Jaxon

The GPS says I'm closing in on the cabin. I don't know what I'm going to do if he's hurt her. I feel so helpless I could choke.

"I'm coming, Olivia," I mutter, downshifting before taking a tight turn in the road.

My whole body is intent on one thing: finding my girl. I have to believe she's okay, that Ryder and I will find her in time. That she'll still be ours, and healthy and whole.

Because the alternative makes me feel like my insides are completely frozen. I thought I knew what true despair was when Genevieve left. But that was absolutely nothing compared to the thought that Olivia might even get a fucking papercut at the hands of her ex.

I make another turn, then another. This road is so damn long. How much time is left before I get there? My headlights illuminate the lines of the road, and the edges of the trees at either side. I ease quickly around another tight turn.

A small figure is in the road in front of me, her pale face illuminated by my car's headlights. *Olivia.* I slam on the brakes just as she jumps out of the way.

I swing open my door and leap from the car. "Olivia!"

"Jaxon?" she asks, holding up a hand to fight off the glare of the lights.

"It's me, baby." I can barely talk, I'm so relieved, but she needs me to be strong.

She stumbles toward me, limping, and I rush to meet her and gather her in my arms. Her grip is strong on my shoulders, but she's shaking so hard her teeth are chattering.

"I pushed him down the stairs," she says. "He's alive, he could be coming at any second."

"I'll deal with him," I say, my voice a growl.

"No, don't let me go," she whispers, holding tighter to me.

A new set of headlights floods the road and Olivia blinks against them. The car stops, and Terrence and Ryder jump out.

"You found her," Ryder says in a rush of air. "Olivia, are you okay? Did he hurt you?"

"I'm okay," she says.

He meets my gaze over the top of her head, a fierce light in his eyes. He wants to kill that asshole. I do, too. I want to make sure he can never touch Olivia again. I don't even want the shape of her name in his mind.

But before I can voice any of the violence lurching through my mind, Terrence speaks up.

"Where is he?"

"Bottom of the stairs, I hope," Olivia says. "He was unconscious and I left him behind, hoping to find a neighbor."

There are no neighbors out here for miles, not on property like Daniel's family owns. It's lucky as fuck that Olivia got out and that we were already on our way. I hate to think what would've happened if we hadn't found her.

"We need to call the police," Ryder says, "immediately. Before I do something to get me thrown in jail."

He's right. I dial Carl Baldwin, my friend at the police station. "We'll give a report tomorrow," I say, "but Olivia was kidnapped by her ex."

"Fuck." He sighs. "The asswipe with the restraining order?"

"Yes. He's knocked out in his lake cabin, and our guy will be on the scene to make sure he doesn't go anywhere."

"If she gives a report and we have you as a witness, we'll be able to put him away this time. He won't be bothering her anymore. His father won't be able to buy him out of this one."

"Good."

I give Baldwin the cabin's address and whatever other pieces of information he asks for, but most of my focus is on the woman in my arms. She's quiet, but shaking slightly, and I run my free hand over her arm, trying to warm her.

As soon as I get off the phone with Baldwin, I say, "We need to go to the cabin, secure the kidnapper."

Olivia flinches in my arms.

I continue, "I'm staying outside in this car with Olivia. Ryder and Terrence, can you two—"

"We'll handle it," Ryder says, violent delight shining in his blue eyes.

I help Olivia into the passenger seat of my car and turn to face Ryder. "Carl Baldwin is coming soon with some officers. I know you want to beat him senseless—trust me, I do, too. But just restrain him. Olivia doesn't want to be visiting you in prison, and neither do I."

Ryder and Terrence climb into Ryder's SUV and tear down the road. The cabin is two minutes away, and I pull into the driveway right after them.

Olivia and I remain in the quiet shell of my car. Olivia looks straight ahead. I watch, gripping the steering wheel tightly, while Ryder and Terrence rush into the house. A part of me wants to go in there and rip Daniel apart. But the bigger, better part of me—the part of me that came alive when Olivia came into my life—wants nothing more than to be here with her.

"You okay, Babydoll?" I ask.

She nods, but she doesn't shift her attention from the windshield.

"You forgot the lesson I gave you," I say. "It might mean you need another spanking."

Blinking slowly, she turns to me. "I don't think you should do that to me anymore."

I can only imagine what she's going through. Kidnapped by her ex. And before that, she'd thought we were rejecting her. Yet a shot of anger works its way through my veins.

"Your lesson was that talking is important. You remember that lesson?"

She nods.

"Because you didn't talk to us," I say, "I spent all evening wondering why you would run out the way you did. Ryder and I puzzled over it. Our only conclusion was that you overheard his side of our conversation on the phone, and you came to a conclusion of your own."

She looks at me now, really looks at me, her gray eyes filling with tears. "You don't want me."

I want to punch the steering wheel or the dashboard or whatever's in reach, but I don't want to scare her. "You are entirely wrong. I do want you. Ryder does, too."

She doesn't roll her eyes, but I can see she wants to.

Reaching out, I touch her chin, turn her face to me. "Eye contact, Olivia. I need you to understand this and pay attention. Ryder and I were talking about Lisa Albertson. Not you."

"But he...he said *I* don't deserve you."

"He said you don't deserve to be harassed by every person you come into contact with. Not his exact words, but that's what he meant. He—and I—are angry that in trying to keep you safe, we put you in more danger from her."

She pushes my hand away and hides her face. "So I caused all of this trouble."

Reaching over, I unbuckle her seatbelt. She doesn't fight me when I lift her up and over to my lap. I push my seat back enough to hold her comfortably, so the steering wheel won't bruise her side.

"I bet Daniel was just waiting for his chance. At some point, he might have found it. Nobody got hurt, except for him. Okay? Don't blame yourself."

"I feel like an idiot."

I tug her hands away from her face and make her look at me again. Then I meld my lips to hers, tasting her lips, kissing her cheeks that are salty from the tears she must have cried tonight.

From the corner of my eye, I see movement as Ryder comes out of the cabin. Keeping my arms around Olivia, I open my door.

"He's all tied up. Still unconscious," Ryder says.

I nod. "Terrence is fine with babysitting him until the police arrive?"

"Yeah."

Olivia is quiet in my lap. I don't want to let her go, not even for a second.

"I'm leaving my car," I say. "Terrence can take it back to the city when he's done here. Will you drive us home?"

"The penthouse, or my cabin?" he asks. "My cabin's closer."

"Where do you want to go, Olivia?" I ask.

"The cabin," she says. "I'd like to see it."

"Gotcha," Ryder says. His gaze is on Olivia as he says in a gentle voice, "Fifteen minutes, we'll be there and you can rest."

I climb out of the car with Olivia and get her settled in the back seat with me, buckling her into the center seat so she's close. She snuggles into my arms, and her hand falls to my thigh. It's too calculated a move to be an accident. Her thumb is about three inches from my dick. I look down and see that she's peeking at me through her eyelashes.

"You want something, Babydoll?" I ask.

Ryder climbs into the driver seat and Olivia glances away from me again.

As soon as Ryder starts the car, I blast the heater and say, "Take off your jeans, Babydoll."

11

Ryder

Olivia's soft gasp of surprise makes my dick hard, and I peek back at her and Jaxon in the rearview mirror. Her face is illuminated by the dash lights, just enough for me to see her scandalized expression.

"But, Daddy," she says in a sweet little whine.

Fuck, what I wouldn't give to hear her calling me *daddy* like that.

"Pants off, Babydoll," he says again, in a voice that tells her he expects obedience.

It takes all my willpower to keep my eyes on the road when she starts squirming, shimmying out of her jeans. Then it gets quiet in the back seat. I think about her panty-clad ass warming the leather and I risk another glance in the rearview.

Her mouth is slack, her gray eyes glazed.

"Your pussy feels so good around my finger," Jaxon says. "I can't wait until it's squeezing my cock."

I could probably use my dick to steer the damn car at this point, it's hard enough. I focus on driving, or I try to, even though my ears can't shut out Olivia's needy moans.

"Fuck, what a good girl you are, Babydoll," Jaxon says.

After what feels like an eternity, I pull into my cabin's driveway. Looking into the rearview again, I catch Olivia looking at *me*. Quickly, I return my attention to the driveway, guiding the car home and then parking.

No sooner have I taken the keys from the ignition than Jaxon's unbuckling Olivia and himself. There's the sound of a zipper and I know he's freeing his dick. I do the same—the pressure against my jeans is too fucking much.

"Face forward when you sit on me, Babydoll," he says.

"But—"

There's the sound of a swat. "I'm not asking you, I'm telling you."

Nothing can pull my attention from the rearview mirror. Her eyes are bright as they find mine. The dash lights are off, but the porch light illuminates her face and body.

I take my cock from my jeans and stroke it slowly. The scent of Olivia's arousal is a heady perfume, filling the car.

Her mouth falls open and I imagine it's because she's finally dropped into place on Jaxon's cock. Sure enough, her body rises and falls as he thrusts into her. His hands come up and he cups her tits over her shirt.

"Take her shirt off," I rasp through gritted teeth.

Olivia sends me an indignant look as Jaxon does what

I asked, lifting her shirt over her head before tossing it aside. Now her tits are encased only in a lacy, sheer bra. He pinches her nipples and her eyes squeeze shut.

"Open your eyes," I say.

She whimpers, but obeys. Her eyes are dark with desperate lust. From over her shoulder, Jaxon gives me a nod of approval.

I can't fucking believe we're doing this again. I've been trying to maintain my distance, trying to keep myself from getting attached, trying not to fall in love with Olivia's mind and body.

My world narrows to Olivia rocking up and down on Jaxon in the back seat, and the throbbing pressure in my cock as I slide my hand over the skin, each stroke heightening the pleasure.

"That's it, Babydoll," Jaxon encourages her. "Lift up and down on Daddy's cock like a good girl. Let me feel your pretty cunt so tight around me."

Her forehead wrinkles and her lips are parted as she gasps, sucking in air and making gorgeous, desperate noises.

"Are you watching Mr. Ryder in that mirror, sweetheart?" Jaxon asks.

"Yes," she says on a drawn-out whimper.

"Good girl."

My hand is moving over my cock automatically—I'm not even controlling my arm anymore. My entire body is a slave to this moment, with the single goal of getting off.

Her moans are louder and her movements more rigid, faster, so I can tell her orgasm is close. I'm about to blow my load and already I know it's gonna be fucking exquisite because she's there behind me, her gaze locked on mine in the mirror, and her face shows wanton, unadulterated lust. If I was back there right now, my cock would be stuffed in her mouth and she'd be greedily gulping around it.

Olivia lets out a long, loud cry and seizes up in Jaxon's lap, her tits held fast in his hands, hard nipples peeking out between his knuckles.

Pleasure rockets through me, concentrating at the base of my spine, my balls almost as hard as my dick. Then it explodes, and I catch my come in my hand.

Jaxon grunts, and I know he's coming, too. I've heard him often enough with Olivia, and before her, with other women we've entertained together. His head is bowed against her back and her body rises and falls as he pumps the last of it into her.

Olivia sags forward, resting her head against the back of my seat. I can smell her sweet candy scent and my dick is already coming to life again.

She reaches forward and rests her palm against my cheek for a brief second. Too brief. I want her skin on mine always. I close my eyes, savoring the contact, until she pulls away.

"Let's go, Babydoll," Jaxon says. "We'll get you tucked in bed."

"I want to sleep with you tonight, Daddy," she says.

"Like you had another option?" he asks.

I open my eyes in time to see him kiss her on top of her head, then he opens the car door.

Olivia doesn't need to put her clothes on—there are no neighbors for miles. He climbs out, fastens his pants, then picks her up. He can get into the house on his own, so I stay behind the wheel, collecting my thoughts.

Olivia lifts her head to peer over his shoulder at me.

She knows something changed here in the car. She has to know. If nothing else, this has shown her how she affects me.

What she does with that information could be my undoing.

Jaxon

Olivia's sleeping, her head on my shoulder, one of her legs thrown over my thighs.

I think back to last night in the back of Ryder's car. Her sounds, the way her body writhed against mine, the sweet glove of her pussy flexing around my cock, her breasts in my hands, pebbled nipples responding to every one of my pinches.

All three of us had needed that interlude. Olivia, because she needed the security of knowing that not only do I still want her, but Ryder does, too—even if the stubborn asshole still won't admit it in any real way. And Ryder and I had needed it to cement the fact that she's safe, and she's with us.

No one is going to take her from us again.

No more miscommunications, no more insecurities, no more of her feeling inadequate. She's more than adequate—she's perfect. Gazing down at her now, at her face relaxed in sleep, her eyelashes touching her cheek and her lips open just slightly, I'm filled with an unfamiliar feeling of warmth through my chest, like my very heart is giving off heat and light.

She's beautiful. Precious.

I don't know what I would do without her in my life. I very nearly had to find out, and the thought fills me with an incapacitating cocktail of rage and sorrow. I chase away the negative feelings by feasting my gaze on her lovely face once more.

Ryder is moving around in the kitchen, and I smell coffee. I wonder if he slept at all last night. I wonder how much our car scene freaked him out.

He needs to get over his barriers. Olivia is *not* Genevieve. There's a purity in Olivia that Genevieve didn't have. Olivia has no affectations, no hidden strategies or manipulations. It took me months to figure out what Genevieve had done to us, carefully disassembling our friendship, brick by brick. It wasn't a demolishment, like it had felt at first, but a calculated undertaking.

The end game? I still have no fucking clue. Maybe she just liked playing games, I don't know.

My phone buzzes with a text, then a second one right away. I growl in irritation. It's probably Carl Baldwin, wanting that report. I think about ignoring it, but then the phone buzzes a third time, and I don't want it to wake Olivia.

Carefully, I lift her leg and slide out from underneath it. I reach my phone just as it buzzes a fourth time. I hate it when people text rapidly again and again. Genevieve used to do it all the time and I tolerated it because I'd thought, at the time, that I loved her.

The phone buzzes a fifth time.

"For fuck's sake, Baldwin," I mutter under my breath as I hurry to the hallway. "What could be so damn important?"

Only when I'm in the hall do I look at the screen. It takes me a moment to really read the name there, because my brain doesn't want to process the information.

It's not Carl Baldwin who's been texting, it's Genevieve.

THANK you for reading *Sinful Restraint*, the first collection of Their Babydoll!

The second collection, *Filthy Restraint*, is available now on your favorite retailer! Visit https://calistajayne.com/filthy-restraint/ for links and info.

ACKNOWLEDGMENTS

As always, I am indebted to the beautiful readers in the Babydolls Club. You bring me so much joy. *mwah!*

A special shout-out goes to our Sweethearts: Jamie G, Claudia, Athena Marie, Elizabeth P, Siobhanmom40, Sarah Kruger-Padgett, Kylilah, and Tina B.

ALSO BY CALISTA JAYNE

Their Rebellious Princess

Their Rebellious Princess

Their Naughty Princess

Their Ruined Princess

Their Beloved Princess

~

My Vampire Doms

Ouch! My Vampire Doms Keep Biting Me

Ouch! My Vampire Doms Don't Sparkle

Ouch! My Vampire Doms Built a Scary Dungeon

Ouch! My Vampire Doms Have Really Long…Fangs

Ouch! My Vampire Doms Give Good Spankings

Ouch! My Vampire Doms Stole My Heart

~

Their Little Liar

Filthy Fiction

Dirty Diction

Tempting Tales

Naughty Novels

~

Their Babydoll

Daddies' Girl

Daddies' Babydoll

Daddies' Little Angel

Daddies' Princess

Daddies' Sweetheart

Daddies Ever After

~

Cinderella's Daddies

Falling for Them

Kneeling for Them

Submitting to Them

Belonging to Them

~

Fiercely Filthy Fairy Tales

Little Red's Temptation

Rapunzel's Sweet Release

~

Babydolls Standalones

Playing by Their Rules

Daddies' Little Troublemaker

ABOUT THE AUTHOR

Calista Jayne adores filthy, smutty romances featuring dominant-yet-tender men. When not writing or reading, she's falling in love with the heroes in K-dramas or walking along a California beach.

Join Calista's newsletter to get showered in love notes (also known as newsletters and updates about new releases and sales) and receive a free book. Visit https://calistajayne.com/babydolls-newsletter to sign up!

Better yet, you can pamper yourself like the princess you are by joining Calista's Babydolls Club. Find everything you need to know here: https://calistajayne.com/club